Somethi
at him.

M000073699

He wasn't watching the fire. He was looking at her. "More wine?"

"No, thank you." Her heart began to pound.

"Then let's move this." Picking up the tray, he lifted it over his knees and set it down on his other side. "It's in the way."

"Of what?" As if she didn't know. As if she didn't recognize the heat that simmered in his eyes.

He took both her hands in his. "Ever since Badger left, I've wanted to kiss you." He stroked the backs of her hands with his thumbs.

She swallowed. "Ever since Badger left, I've been hoping you would."

Releasing her hands, he cupped her face and gazed into her eyes. "Good to know." Urging her closer with easy pressure, he placed a soft kiss on her forehead.

She closed her eyes, heart thrumming, as his butterfly kisses brushed her eyelids, then her cheeks. He lingered there, igniting little bursts of pleasure with each caress.

As he gently kissed the corners of her mouth, she quivered in anticipation. *Soon.* Then his warm lips settled over hers.

A COWBOY'S KISS

THE MCGAVIN BROTHERS

Vicki Lewis Thompson

Ocean Dance Press

A COWBOY'S KISS
© 2018 Vicki Lewis Thompson

ISBN: 978-1-946759-34-4

Ocean Dance Press LLC
PO Box 69901
Oro Valley, AZ 85737

All Rights Reserved. No part of this book may be
used or reproduced or transmitted in any form or
by any means, graphic, electronic, or mechanical,
including photocopying, recording, taping, or by
any information storage or retrieval system,
without the written permission of the publisher
except in the case of brief quotations embodied in
critical articles or reviews.

This is a work of fiction. Any resemblance to
actual persons, living or dead, business
establishments, events, or locales is entirely
coincidental.

Cover art by Kristin Bryant

Visit the author's website at
VickiLewisThompson.com

Want more cowboys? Check out these other titles by
Vicki Lewis Thompson

The McGavin Brothers
A Cowboy's Strength
A Cowboy's Honor
A Cowboy's Return
A Cowboy's Heart
A Cowboy's Courage
A Cowboy's Christmas

Thunder Mountain Brotherhood
Midnight Thunder
Thunderstruck
Rolling Like Thunder
A Cowboy Under the Mistletoe
Cowboy All Night
Cowboy After Dark
Cowboy Untamed
Cowboy Unwrapped
In the Cowboy's Arms
Say Yes to the Cowboy
Do You Take This Cowboy?

Sons of Chance
Wanted!
Ambushed!
Claimed!
Should've Been a Cowboy
Cowboy Up
Cowboys Like Us
Long Road Home
Lead Me Home
Feels Like Home

1

Luke Bennett cursed under his breath. He should have believed the weather report instead of the clear sky that had lured him to Bozeman. But the sale at a local housewares store ended this weekend and he'd wanted a set of dishes.

Got the dishes. Was gonna be late to his three o'clock appointment at the Guzzling Grizzly. The white stuff spraying his windshield meant he had to slow to a crawl or risk an accident. He hated being late.

The weather was a piss-poor excuse for lateness, too. If he'd left earlier...hang on. Some critter was on the median. Hard to identify what it was with the snow coming down so fast. Wolf? Coyote?

No, looked more like...shit-fire, it ran right in front of him. Clearly a black dog, trotting along the shoulder. On a mission. In the middle of nowhere.

He eased to the side of the road, keeping the animal in the beam of his headlights. Edging over a little more, he put on his hazards. If he got stuck in the snow...well, he just wouldn't. He set the emergency brake before leaning across the console and opening the passenger door. "Hey, boy!"

The dog paused and looked back before continuing down the side of the road.

"Not gonna make this easy, are you, sport?" His boots sank into a snowdrift as he climbed out. He kept his attention on the dog as he plowed to the front of the truck.

When he whistled through his teeth, the animal stopped again and turned in his direction. He patted his thigh. "C'mere, boy!" Had to respect the caution of that critter. Cold, lost, likely hungry, with icicles forming on his coat, and he still wasn't ready to run into the arms of the first guy who came along.

"It's okay!" He crouched down and held out his hand. "Let me take you someplace warm."

The dog took a tentative step toward him, then another. It was mostly black, with a big white patch on its chest.

"That's it! Keep coming, buddy. I won't hurt you." Snow melted on his cheeks and eyelashes.

He hadn't taken time to put on his hat or button his coat. His hair was soon plastered to his head and wet flakes soaked his shirt. But moving now could spook the dog and send it running off. It likely would freeze to death when the temperature dropped tonight.

The gap between them slowly closed. Poor critter was shivering. Luke had watched a TV show about border collies a while ago. This dog looked similar—same size, floppy ears, white and black coat. "Come on, boy! Let's get in the warm truck. I have a nice cozy blanket waiting for you."

At last the dog got close enough to sniff his outstretched hand. And lick it.

This might work. Luke stroked the icy fur and scratched behind the floppy ears. "It'd be best if I carry you back to the truck, buddy. Will you let me?"

Still trembling, the dog gazed into his eyes with a combination of anxiety and hope.

"Let's go, sport." Scooping the quivering animal into his arms, he hoisted him up and draped him around his shoulders. He'd expected some resistance, but instead the dog settled in as if used to being carried like this.

The animal didn't behave like a stray. How had it ended up alone on the highway in a snowstorm? He got the shivering dog onto the passenger seat and closed the door. He'd left the motor running so heat poured from the vents.

By the time he slid behind the wheel, the dog had curled up on the seat. But it was still shaking and the worried expression in those brown eyes broke his heart. A soft whine was followed by a slight tail wag.

"Poor doggie. Let's get you dried off." Moving slowly, he reached behind the seat for a blanket. "This'll help." Laying it over the ice-encrusted coat, he rubbed gently. "You've been out here a while, haven't you, pup?"

The whine was a little louder and the thump of the dog's tail more animated.

"Don't you worry. I'll find out where you belong." As the cab warmed, the critter gradually relaxed and heaved a deep sigh.

Luke reversed the blanket to the dry side and tucked it snugly around the dog's body. Then he retrieved his phone from the console. Michael didn't answer, so he left a message and put the phone back in the console.

"Here we go, pup. We'll be in Eagles Nest before you know it. Ten minutes, fifteen, tops." He put the truck in gear and eased back onto the deserted highway.

The dog scrambled to a sitting position and the blanket fell away.

"Easy boy." Yikes. If the pup got agitated...but no, not a problem. An ear flicked in his direction, but otherwise the dog's attention remained on the road ahead.

"Seasoned traveler, are you?" Thank God for small favors. "That's good, because I'm fresh out of dog crates and I couldn't put you in the back because it's snowing."

The animal gave him a quick glance before focusing on the highway.

Luke smiled. What expressive eyes. That look clearly said *I know it's snowing, genius.* "So, pup, I'm asking myself what a smart critter like you is doing on a highway in a snowstorm."

The flick of those black, floppy ears was the only indication the dog was listening.

"And no collar and tags. I'm hoping for a microchip. You got a microchip, buddy?"

The pup glanced at him again before standing and executing a head-to-tail shake, spraying water everywhere.

"Hey." Luke wiped a hand over his dripping face. "Sit down, buddy."

Immediately the dog's haunches dropped.

"Well-trained, too, looks like. Somebody must be worried sick about you, sport. I just have to find that person so you can get on with your life."

That comment netted him a doggie smile—mouth slightly open, pink tongue visible. Cute as hell. How anybody could lose a good dog like this one was beyond him.

Moments later he parked in front of the Guzzling Grizzly. Not many vehicles in the parking lot, which had been the plan. Michael co-owned the GG but he also tended bar on Sundays. He'd chosen a slow time for their meeting.

Luke turned off the engine and unfastened his seat belt. "Hang tight for a minute, pup. Let me ask if I can bring you in."

Quickly exiting the truck, he dashed through the falling snow and into the GG. Country music served as background this time of day. Come tonight, though, Bryce McGavin and Nicole Williams would take the stage and the place would be hopping.

Only two tables were occupied now and no one sat at the bar, a gleaming dark-wood beauty that had to be close to a hundred and fifty years old.

Michael came out from behind it, hand outstretched. "You made it. What's this about a dog?"

"He's waiting in the truck." Luke returned the handshake. "I didn't want to bring him in without asking."

"Hey, go ahead. Let's take him back to the office. While you bring him in I'll round up some food and water."

"That would be great. I'm sure he's hungry. Be right back." Luke jogged to the truck and paused. No collar. No leash. He shrugged and opened the passenger door.

"I'll have to carry you in, pup." Getting the dog settled around his shoulders was easier the second time. He nudged the truck door closed with his knee. So far, so good.

But getting through the GG's front door while keeping a grip on the dog would be a trick. Then a woman in a blue parka with a large shopping bag in one hand dashed in front of him.

"I'll get the door."

"Thank you, ma'am. Much obliged." He walked through ahead of her in total violation of the cowboy code. It couldn't be helped.

The woman followed him as he carried the dog back to the office.

"Is the dog hurt?"

"Don't think so, ma'am. Likely just hungry and thirsty."

"Not yours, then?"

"No, ma'am."

"Beautiful dog."

"Sure is."

Michael came out of the kitchen holding two large pasta dishes.

As the dog began to quiver, Luke tightened his grip. Must have smelled the food. "Stay put, boy."

Michael paused. "Hey, Abigail! Didn't expect to see you today."

"I know. Never mind me. Give that poor dog some food."

"Sure thing." Michael went into the office and put down the bowls. "There you go, puppy dog."

Luke set the animal down and expected a mad dash for the food bowl. Instead the dog looked up at him as if asking permission. His heart turned over. "Go ahead, boy. Go eat."

The dog walked to the food bowl and began gulping down the hamburger.

"Hey, thanks, Michael. Looks like he needed that."

"No worries. Listen, one of my servers is out sick so I have to go check on a customer. Be right back."

"Sure thing." Luke watched the dog lick the bowl clean and move over to the water bowl next to it.

"Wow, hungry dog."

"Yes, ma'am." Luke glanced over at the woman Michael had called Abigail. Her name was familiar.

She pushed back her hood to reveal a mop of short, curly brown hair. "Yet that pup wasn't going to eat until you said okay. Amazing."

"I know. Somebody trained him really well."

"Or her."

"I guess it could be a her. I just assumed..."

She laughed. "With that fluffy coat, it would be hard to tell, especially if the dog's a neutered male."

"Guess so." What an odd conversation to be having with a woman he'd just met. Whoops. He'd failed to introduce himself. His mother would have his hide for a slip like that. "I'm Luke Bennett, by the way."

"Abigail Summers." She held out her hand. "I own the—"

"Pie in the Sky Bakery." He clasped her hand. Her grip was firm, probably from kneading dough. "I was trying to remember where I'd heard your name. I've only been in once with my folks over Christmas vacation to pick up a few breakfast pastries. I don't remember seeing you."

"I was probably delivering pies and bread to the GG. That was a super busy time."

"I'll bet."

"Am I right that you've just relocated from Portland? I seem to remember your mom saying something like that."

He went on alert. His mom was a recovering matchmaker who'd vowed to mend her ways. But if she'd been talking him up to Abigail, then she might have fallen off the wagon. "Did she happen to mention that I'm single?"

"No." She looked amused. "Was she supposed to?"

"No! I just—"

"Wanted me to know you're available?"

"Absolutely not." Heat rose from his collar. "That came out all wrong. I'm not in the market."

"You already have a girlfriend?"

"No, I don't, but—"

"You're looking for a boyfriend?"

"*No.*" He scrubbed a hand over his face. Could this get any worse? His mom had kept her word about not trying to set him up. Explaining her previous irritating behavior to Abigail would get him out of this fix but it wouldn't be gallant.

A bump against his thigh made him glance down. Saved by the dog. The pup stood staring up at him as if he *or she* needed something.

Abigail chuckled. "That look means *I need to go outside.*"

He met her calm gaze. Too bad he was still embarrassed as hell. And now they were discussing the dog's bathroom requirements. "How do you know?"

"My family had dogs when I was growing up. That's the look they give you when they need to take care of business." The corners of her mouth tilted up. "And then you'll know if it's a boy or a girl."

"I don't have a collar and leash."

Opening her coat, she unwound a long scarf from around her neck. "Use this."

"I don't think—"

"Use it." She shook it at him. "Tomorrow you can buy a leash. Today you need to improvise."

"Thank you, ma'am."

"You're welcome."

The scarf worked like a charm. He secured it around the dog's neck and led the critter out the front door and over to an area beside the parking lot. As the dog squatted to relieve herself, he had his answer. He'd rescued a girl.

2

Abigail watched him lead the dog away. Damn, that cowboy was cute. And he'd saved a dog from freezing to death. Cute *and* heroic. Great combo.

After the initial confusion, she'd figured out he wasn't looking for a partner of either gender. He'd seemed worried about what his mom had said, though. Abigail got that. Virginia Bennett loved to talk about her children and was perfectly capable of oversharing.

Now that Abigail's parents were both gone, she didn't have to deal with that problem. Hearing about it made her wistful, though. She would put up with a little oversharing if she could have her folks back.

Michael reappeared, wiping his hands with a bar towel. Good-looking and gregarious, he was a perfect co-owner for the GG. "Where's Luke?"

"The dog needed to go out."

"Oh. So why did you come over on your day off?"

"Frank said he was out of pies." She held up the oversized shopping bag she'd brought. "So I baked him some."

"I'm sure he didn't expect you to do that ASAP."

"I know, but I hate to think of anyone running out of something and disappointing customers."

He shrugged. "We run out of stuff all the time. It's impossible to gauge exactly what you'll need."

"Which is why I always make more than I need."

"Well, Frank doesn't operate that way. He—oh, look who's back. Nice dog collar, Luke."

"Abigail loaned me her scarf."

She waved a hand at the dog. "You can keep it for now. What do you have, boy or girl?"

"Girl."

Michael grinned. "Guess taking a dog out to do its business would give you that info. What're you going to name her?"

"Nothing."

"Nothing?" Michael frowned. "That's a terrible name. She'll get a complex."

"I mean I'm not naming her because I intend to find out where she belongs. She's a great dog and someone is missing her like crazy."

Michael surveyed the dog. "Correct me if I'm wrong, but you had to use Abigail's scarf because this pup has no collar or tags."

"True, but she could be microchipped."

"How could you tell if she is or not?"

"I don't know, but there must be a way."

"I'll bet there is." Abigail pulled a phone out of her pocket. "Let's find out."

"You should give her a name, Luke."

"But if she has a name and what I call her isn't even close, then what? I'll just confuse her."

"Maybe, but—"

"What I could use is a couple pounds of hamburger to get me through until tomorrow. If I could buy some from you I'd be grateful."

"Sure. Glad to help."

Abigail glanced up from her phone. "Use a stud finder. That will tell you if she's chipped or not. If she is, it should be somewhere between her shoulder blades."

"Just so happens I have a stud finder." Michael walked over to the desk and pulled open a drawer. "Needed it when I hung up the Murphy coat of arms." He gestured toward the wall.

Abigail gazed at the heavy wooden plaque. "That's cool. Is it new?"

"Just arrived." He handed Luke the stud finder. "Bryce ordered the McGavin one after he saw mine."

Luke smiled. "I'll just bet he did. But why not hang them in the bar so everyone can see them?"

"We talked about it, but the GG is all about Old West nostalgia. Wouldn't fit."

"Guess not." Luke crouched down and ran the stud finder over the dog's shoulders. "Not finding a chip in there, pup."

She wagged her tail.

"She likes you," Abigail said.

"The feeling's mutual." He stood and returned Michael's stud finder. "Thanks. Tomorrow I'll contact the local rescue organizations in the area and give them a description."

Michael nodded. "That's about all you can do. Listen, I'm thinking we should reschedule our consultation. Customers are starting to come in and we've lost our window of opportunity."

Luke sighed. "I know. My fault and I apologize."

"No worries. How's Wednesday at three?"

"Let me check." He pulled out his phone. "I'm free."

"Let's do it then. My business plan can wait a couple more days."

"I appreciate your patience. If you can bring me that hamburger, I'll get out of your way."

"Be right back." Michael paused in the doorway of the office. "Is two pounds enough?"

"Plenty. I'll go shopping first thing tomorrow."

"Okay, then." Michael headed for the kitchen.

"I didn't know you were a business consultant." Abigail hadn't been given that tidbit. "The way your mom described your old job, I thought you might be a chef."

He grinned. "Don't have much talent for cooking. I handled their marketing, financial projections, things like that."

"And then decided to go out on your own?"

"Yes, ma'am."

Running into him like this was a golden opportunity if she had the nerve to take it. She tamped down a surge of anxiety. "I just might need your services." There. She'd opened the door.

"I could give you my card if you'd like to think about—"

"I don't need to think about it." In for a penny, in for a pound. "I've been thinking about getting some advice but I didn't know where to go. You're local. I like that."

"Local is what I'm concentrating on. I could help you tweak your business plan and—"

"I don't have one."

He blinked. "Didn't the bank require it?"

"I paid cash for everything."

"I see." He hesitated. "A business plan is still a good thing to have."

"I realize that. But I didn't know who to ask, who to trust."

"Then I'm honored you're willing to trust me."

She smiled. "Your dad's a beloved minister in town and your mom's a regular customer at Pie in the Sky. You just rescued this poor dog. I think I can trust you."

"Well, when you put it that way..." He grinned. "When do you want to get together?"

"How about Tuesday afternoon after I close the bakery? Do you have an opening at four?"

He pulled out his phone. "I sure do. Four on Tuesday, then."

"What's your favorite cookie?"

"Oh, you don't have to—"

"Sure I do. I want you to appreciate what a fine baker I am. Won't that affect your calculations?"

"Cookies always affect my calculations. My favorite is peanut butter cookies. The kind you mash down with a fork."

"I use a mallet, but the idea's the same. Be prepared for the best peanut butter cookies you've ever tasted."

"That's a challenge. My mom's are pretty good."

That gave her pause. Surpassing his mom's baking expertise wasn't her goal. "Then let's forget those. What kind of cookie do you love that your mom doesn't make often?"

"Oatmeal raisin. She doesn't like raisins."

"Then that's what I'll make for you. See you at four on Tuesday."

* * *

What had she been thinking? Abigail blamed the appeal of a rugged cowboy with a rescued dog draped across his broad shoulders. Yes, she had some financial issues, but she wasn't ready to discuss them with anyone, let alone a professional.

Yet who better to help her than a professional? Who cared if he was a brown-eyed, muscular dreamboat with a heart of gold? He had the expertise to tell her how to solve her problem. She had business galore and she was in the red every single month. Soon the inheritance from her parents would be gone. Unless she turned things around, her business would fail.

But she didn't want Luke to know that she was in dire straits. She'd rather have him think of her as a slightly disorganized but highly creative business owner. A few tips from him, and she'd be right as rain.

The self-talk wasn't helping. Fifteen minutes before Luke was due to arrive, she'd burned the oatmeal-raisin cookies she'd made for him and was frantically mixing up a new batch.

Her other employees were gone, but Ingrid, her apprentice baker, was wiping down the bistro tables. Although Ingrid was off at one, she often came down from her apartment upstairs to help close.

Abigail lived upstairs, too, a convenient arrangement when she had to get up in the wee hours of the morning to start baking. The third apartment had been leased several months ago by a graphic designer named Roxanne.

"Are you okay?" Ingrid finished cleaning the last table and walked back to the open kitchen area. "I don't usually hear you swear."

"I just wish I hadn't made this appointment. I don't have time to deal with creating a business plan right now."

"You don't have a business plan?"

"Not written down." She spooned the batter onto a cookie sheet.

"It's in your head?"

"Sort of."

"That doesn't sound very scientific." Ingrid tidied the bun she wore to keep her blond hair under control during work hours.

"But it's organic. It's flexible. Much better than spelling it out on paper and creating some anal manifesto I feel obliged to adhere to." She glanced up when Ingrid started to laugh. "What?"

"Can I hide in the pantry during your meeting? I want to hear you say that to your business consultant."

"I won't say that to him. I'm only saying it to you. And I don't see what's so funny." She put the cookies in the oven and remembered to set the timer.

"I know you don't. That's why your concept is so adorable. But you asked this guy to come over today, so you must know in your heart that you need a more structured plan."

"I suppose I do." She rinsed out the stainless steel mixing bowl and put it into the large capacity dishwasher. "Did you take the leftovers in the case for you and Roxanne?"

"Not yet, but I will. She mentioned something about movie night at her place. Think you can stay awake through a full-length feature?"

"I'll do my best."

"I'll pinch you so you'll stay awake." Ingrid's gaze darted to the sidewalk outside the bakery's windows. "Don't look now, but a tall cowboy is headed our way. He's carrying a laptop case over his shoulder. I should take off."

Abigail's heart began to pound. "Please don't desert me."

"But—"

"Not yet, anyway. Stay and meet him. Besides, you didn't box up the leftovers."

"I can do that after he leaves." The chime sounded as the front door opened and Ingrid's attention flicked to the front of the store. "Oh, wow, he is a cutie-pie," she murmured. "Is that why you set this up?"

"No, but it didn't hurt."

"Thought so."

"Come on. I'll introduce you." Putting on her happy face, Abigail walked around the counter. "Hi, Luke! Right on time. I'd like you to meet my assistant, Ingrid Lindstrom."

He swept off his hat. "Pleased to meet you, Ingrid."

"Same here." Ingrid shook his hand. "Your dad's a hoot, by the way."

"He's an original and I'm proud to be his son. Even when he appears in a spandex superhero outfit in public."

Ingrid laughed. "You mean the Christmas talent show?"

"You were there."

"We both were," Abigail said. "I can't wait to find out what he comes up with next year. Listen, if you'd like to leave your laptop on a bistro table, I can take your jacket. We have a—"

"Coat tree. I see it." He put down his laptop and unbuttoned his sheepskin jacket as he walked over to the corner of the room. "Something sure smells good."

"Cookies," Abigail said.

"Oatmeal-raisin?"

"You've got it."

"Great." He took off his jacket, which provided a nice view of broad shoulders in a chambray yoked shirt and jeans that cupped a firm ass.

Ingrid gave her a nudge and mouthed *Oh, my God.*

Abigail ducked her head so he wouldn't come back and find her grinning like a fool.

He propped his hat on the same hook where he'd hung his jacket and started back toward them. "All decked out for Valentine's Day, I see."

Both Abigail and Ingrid blurted out answers and then tripped over each other apologizing for interrupting. No telling how long that nonsense would have continued if the oven timer hadn't dinged.

Abigail swallowed her laughter and looked at her friend. "Cookies are done."

"I'll take them out." Ingrid's voice was unnaturally high, as if she could barely keep from cracking up. With a muffled snort, she hurried into the kitchen.

Luke gestured to the front window. "I like the painted Valentine's Day scene."

"That's Roxanne's handiwork." Abigail drew in a calming breath. "She's a graphic artist."

"An employee?"

"No, a friend. She lives in one of the apartments upstairs."

"She did a good job."

"She did. She helped us with the other decorations, too. It's a major holiday for a bakery so we wanted to capitalize on it." His gorgeousness quotient seemed to increase with every minute he stood there.

"I'm sure a bakery's popular this time of year. People love their sweets."

His mouth was especially nice. Full and sensuous. Better stop staring at it. "I've found that individual desserts work better than full-sized ones. They're fun to make, too. I think of them as little slices of heaven."

"Can you give me some examples?"

"Oh, like mini heart-shaped chocolate cakes, heart-shaped chocolate cookies with pink frosting, chocolate frosted eclairs with raspberry filling, strawberry tarts drizzled with dark chocolate..." Was it her imagination or had his brown eyes turned a shade darker? "Does that give you an idea?"

"Sure does." He cleared his throat. "I can tell you love your work."

"It's my passion."

"Obviously." He took a breath and glanced around. "Your open kitchen concept is nice. It lets the customers see the work in progress."

"Like this one." Ingrid came around the counter with a small plate of fragrant cookies. "Can't get any fresher than straight out of the oven. They're still warm." She extended the plate. "Help yourself."

"As if I'd say no." He took a cookie, bit into it, and closed his eyes with a soft moan.

Abigail couldn't resist glancing at Ingrid. Then she quickly looked away before they both lost it. Luke might or might not be good for her business, but he sure as hell was good for her libido.

3

What a fascinating woman. Luke had been mesmerized by Abigail's description of the specialty treats she was making for Valentine's Day. Her enthusiasm for her work was a real turn-on.

Good for her that she'd created a satisfying business that clearly brought her joy. Helping someone with such a positive mindset would be rewarding.

On Sunday afternoon at the GG he would have described her as cute. Today, surrounded by white lace, red hearts and the aroma of cookies, she was in her element. He couldn't stop looking at her.

And she was looking back, her eyes bright with laughter. His reaction to the cookie must have tickled her. Were her eyes brown? Green? Hard to say. But he enjoyed the sparkle.

Ingrid set the plate of cookies on the counter. "Great to meet you, Luke. I'll leave the two of you to continue your discussion while I head upstairs and feed my fish."

"You live upstairs, too?"

"I do. It's convenient."

"I can see how it would be." After she left he looked at Abigail. "Do Roxanne and Ingrid rent from you?"

"Goodness, no. I don't own the building. I lease the space for the bakery plus one of the apartments. There are three up there."

"So you have a landlord."

"Landlady. Mrs. Gibbs."

"Okay then. I was beginning to think you were independently wealthy."

"Hardly. My inheritance was enough for the equipment and a cushion to get me through the first year or so."

Something in her expression told him that cushion might be dwindling. "You've made this place very inviting."

"Thank you. Want a tour?"

"Absolutely. Can I take a cookie for the trip?"

"By all means. Grab the whole plate."

"Don't mind if I do." He picked up the cookies. "These are delicious. Best I've ever had. Did you bake them or Ingrid?"

"I did. She's concentrating on bread and croissants to start with, which is a huge help." She walked around the counter. "Follow me."

He sure was enjoying the cookies. And spending time with Abigail, who was the sort of vivacious, independent woman he was drawn to. His mom would have recognized that. She'd shown great restraint in keeping her mouth shut.

"We have four ovens." Abigail pointed them out. "If I've stockpiled enough inventory, then we never have to run out of anything."

"Not even by the end of the day?" Could
~ potentially wasteful.

"Rarely, especially now that I have Ingrid
to help me. I start at three and bake until we open
at six, when Ingrid pitches in. If pastries are going
fast, we keep baking so we can replenish the
supply." She gestured to a large island in the
center of the kitchen. "Prep area. Pans stored
underneath."

"If you're baking, who waits on
customers?"

"I have two more employees who are
available to work the counter. I schedule one or
both to come in at six, depending on whether it's
Ingrid's day off. Traffic slows down around nine.
We refresh the display cases, sweep the floor,
wipe down the tables, things like that."

"Your other staff members stay during the
slow time?"

"There's no point in sending them home.
Business gets brisk again around ten-thirty when
customers come in for mid-morning snacks. That's
when most people pick up their pies and cakes,
too."

"Do you serve coffee?"

She glanced at him. "I do. Do you want
some?"

"No, thanks. Just wondered how many
people stick around to eat their mid-morning
snacks."

"A few."

"How about afternoons?"

"Some people want a couple of cookies or
a pastry and coffee, but most are buying a whole

pie or cake to take home. Not super busy in the afternoon."

"But you still have three people here?"

"Except when someone's on a break. I stagger those."

He nodded. Sounded like she might be overstaffed but he wasn't ready to get into that. When she showed him the supply room, he had the impression she was overstocked, but he didn't mention that, either.

Better to emphasize the good things and there were plenty of those. "Your setup is great," he said after the tour ended. "The kitchen is well organized and I'll bet customers like being able to watch you at work." He certainly would enjoy it.

"Thanks."

"On top of that, everything's spotless. I'm sure the health inspector loves this place."

Her face lit with pleasure. "We've received excellent reports."

"I need to make some notes, and I'd love some of that coffee, if you're still offering."

"Sure." She grabbed a sturdy white mug and walked over to a large urn. "Cream?"

"No, thanks." He took the full mug she handed him. "Smells great."

"I'm particular about my coffee."

"Will you have some with me?"

"That's actually a good idea." She fetched another mug and filled it with coffee. "I'm hoping to stay up and watch a movie with Ingrid and Roxanne tonight. Usually I fall asleep halfway through." She hoisted her mug. "This will help."

"Yeah, but you still have to get up at three."

"There's that. I usually catch up on Sunday."

"That's a fallacy. Sleep doesn't work that way."

She laughed. "I know. But I pretend it does. Hey, before you get started on your notes, what happened with the dog?"

"I still have her. And that reminds me. I have your scarf in my coat pocket." He set down his mug and walked back to the coat tree.

"Nobody's claimed her?"

"Not so far. The vet said she's healthy and confirmed there's no microchip. I've contacted all the local rescue operations, but I've heard nothing back." He returned with her scarf and handed it to her. "Appreciate the loan. I washed it."

"That was nice of you." She laid it on the counter. "If no one shows up, will you keep her?"

"I'm not thinking about that yet. I don't want to get attached and then have someone show up to claim her."

"Then I'll bet you haven't named her, either."

"No, ma'am."

Her smile was warm. "I completely understand. But good luck keeping your distance. She looked like the kind of dog who would steal your heart."

"Mm." He wasn't going to admit that she already had. "Guess I'd better get to work."

"Do you want me to stay out of your way while you make your notes?"

"Not at all. Please sit with me. That way if I have more questions you'll be right there." And whenever he looked up, he'd be able to see her smiling face.

"All right, then."

The bistro chair was a little small for him, but the coffee, the cookies and the company made up for it. He hauled his laptop out of its case, flipped it open and typed a few sentences to remind him of what he'd seen so far and what he'd investigate as they moved forward.

Then he asked her for a few details—rent payments, utilities, employee wages. Her answers were vague, as if she had no clear idea of those figures and no easily accessible way to check them. When he tried to get an estimate of monthly income, she was even more tentative and seemed to be tensing up.

He shifted gears. "What made you decide to go into this field?"

"Do you need that for your evaluation?"

"No, ma'am. I'm just curious."

"My mom and I used to bake together all the time. She liked it but I *loved* it. In culinary school that was all I ever wanted to work on. After graduation, I got a job at a bakery in Rapid City."

"That's where you're from?"

"Yep."

"So why move here?"

"I didn't want to compete with that bakery and I would have because this one's modeled after it. I love the owner, and intentionally or not, I would have taken some of her customers. Maybe a big portion of them."

"Judging from these cookies and the pastries I had at Christmas, I don't doubt it."

"Besides, after my folks died, I didn't have much reason to stay."

"Oh." That's where the inheritance had come from. He met her gaze. "I'm sorry. I didn't mean to—"

"It's okay." She reached over and touched his arm. "Don't feel bad."

Her touch was brief, but the effect lasted long after she'd moved her hand. He'd wanted her to leave it there. "How long ago?"

"Almost five years. Took me a while to settle the estate. Legalese and paperwork aren't my long suit."

Which meant she needed someone to teach her about those things. "Well, they're mine."

"I'm counting on it." She hesitated. "So what do you think? Should we start working on my business plan today or do you want to take what you have and come back to me with recommendations?"

"That depends on you. I'm guessing you asked for this meeting because you're worried about something. What is it?"

She looked down at her fingers as she laced and unlaced them several times. At last she glanced up at him. "That I'll run out of money."

"Is that a real possibility?"

"Yes. I get plenty of business, but every month I spend more than I make. I've been subsidizing from the money I had left over after buying all the equipment and remodeling the space. But that's getting low. When it's gone…" She shrugged. "I'll be SOL."

He took a deep breath. He'd been afraid of something like this. His job was to stay calm and offer suggestions. "Can you estimate how much longer you could go on at this rate?"

"Three months. Two if something unexpected crops up."

"That gives us some time. Not much, but—"

"Thank you."

"For what? I haven't done anything."

"Yes, you have. You said it gives *us* time. That's huge. Now I don't feel so alone."

Just like that, the relationship turned personal. And warm. Happened fast, too. Made him want to touch her. He didn't. "That's because you're not alone. I'll do everything I can to keep you from going out of business."

She smiled. "Just like you rescued a dog from the highway."

"I consider that completely different."

"I don't. You see a person or an animal in trouble and you want to help."

"Now I'm feeling like the Lone Ranger, which I'm not. I plan to bill you for my services." Even if he'd do it for free. But he knew without asking that she wouldn't allow that.

"It'll be worth every penny if I can keep Pie in the Sky going. I haven't wanted to face the possibility of losing the business, but I have, now, and I'll fight to keep that from happening."

"Good." He'd fight beside her. "Let's start with inventory. How much do you sell of each item each day?"

"I have no idea."

"Seriously?" This was worse than he'd thought.

"Seriously. How am I supposed to keep track of it all?"

"On a computer, paper and pencil, whatever works. But you need to know how much you produce, what goes out the door, and what's left at the end of the day. Your employees can help with counting what goes in the case. Deduct what's left at the end of the day from your totals to figure out how much of each item you sold."

"I guess I could do that."

"That's all I'm asking for now. I'll come back on Saturday afternoon at four and we'll evaluate."

"You don't want to draw up a business plan?"

"Not until we know what's going out the door. We need that measurement before we proceed."

"Like I said, paperwork is not my long suit."

"I understand that. But it's almost impossible to evaluate how a business is doing without some data. You could pay me to come in here for the rest of the week and collect it for you, but that would be very expensive."

Arms crossed, she frowned and stared into space. "I really do hate paperwork."

"You don't have to do it. No one's forcing you." *But don't quit on me before we even get started.*

Her shoulders dropped. "I want you to work on this with me. I'll gather the numbers for you."

"Trust me, Abigail. Once you have a handle on how your business truly operates, you'll be in a much stronger position."

"I'll take your word for it."

"Please do." Glancing at the time on his phone, he reluctantly shoved back his chair. "I should be on my way. I need to pick up the dog at Wild Creek Ranch."

"Kendra's watching her?"

"Yes, ma'am. When I told her about the dog she figured out I was a little worried about leaving the pup alone."

"And she offered to dog-sit. That sounds like Kendra." Abigail stood and he got to his feet, too. "I have a few brownies left in the case and she loves those." Rounding the counter, she walked into the kitchen. "I'll package them up."

"Great idea." He fetched his hat and jacket before returning to the display case. "Thanks for thinking of it."

"I can't help myself. Giving people what I've baked makes me happy." She came back with two flattened boxes.

"But I'm paying for the brownies." He reached for the wallet in his hip pocket.

"Put your money away. Consider it my contribution to your rescue efforts." She quickly assembled one box and transferred the brownies into it.

"Well...thanks." He understood the urge to help only too well. "But what's the other box for?"

"The rest of your cookies."

"For Kendra?"

"No, for you. Kendra prefers chocolate goodies."

"Oh. But I've already eaten at least six, maybe seven."

She paused to give him an amused glance. "Is that your limit?"

"No, ma'am, but—"

"I always intended to send the rest home with you. Please take them with my blessing." She taped both boxes shut and handed them over the counter with a quick smile. "See you on Saturday afternoon."

"Looking forward to it." Understatement. Saturday couldn't come soon enough.

Abigail was talented, hard-working and generous. With his guidance, her business would soon be operating in the black. He lived for challenges like this. The fact that she was extremely appealing was...he laughed at his own joke...icing on the cake.

4

Abigail gathered up all the remaining pastries in the case, tucked them in an oversized box, and locked up the bakery. To access her apartment, she had to go out the front door and in through the door adjacent to it.

A steep set of stairs took her to the second floor. Hers was the largest apartment, with windows facing on the street. Ingrid and Roxanne's apartments both looked out on a back alley, but they also had a view of the mountains.

She texted her friends that she'd brought dessert from downstairs. When Roxanne ordered take-out, like she had tonight, they all shared the cost. They took turns providing wine.

Roxanne had initiated their first get-together a couple of weeks after she'd moved in. She claimed to enjoy the added energy in her apartment since she worked alone so much. Consequently, it had become their gathering place.

Before she changed into her sweats and long-sleeved T-shirt, Abigail put together a list on her computer of all the bakery goods they'd sell in the morning. She'd keep the list behind the counter and ask Yolanda and Doug to take a count before the bakery opened for business. Abigail would keep track of any items she or Ingrid added during the day and note which items were left when they closed.

Yolanda had a knack for detail and would think this was fun. She was taking online classes toward a pharmacy degree. Doug was a nice kid who was only twenty and still figuring out what he wanted from life. He wasn't a self-starter, but he always did what she asked him to do.

By the time Abigail changed clothes and started out the door with the box of bakery goodies, she was starving. She might have missed lunch. She couldn't remember eating anything so she probably hadn't. A short walk down the hall brought her to Roxanne's door. She gave it a quick couple of taps.

Typical Roxanne, she flung it open and pulled Abigail inside without bothering to close it again. "You have to see the new logo I made for Zane McGavin's raptor rescue!" Roxanne had dark, curly hair that turned wild and crazy unless she secured it with a clip or a scrunchie. "I asked him if he wanted a redo and he was all over it. See what you think."

Abigail studied the oval image on the computer screen. Roxanne had chosen to use a pair of eagles in flight above snow-covered mountains. "Beautiful."

"His other logo only had one eagle on it, but a mated pair appealed to me."

"Me, too. Have you shown it to him?"

"Yep! He loved it. And today I also got a commission from an excursion outfit in Antarctica and another one from an upscale hotel in Madrid. The internet is a beautiful thing."

"It sure is for you." Abigail handed her the box of goodies. "Where's Ingrid?"

"Talking to that long-distance boyfriend of hers. I don't get it. Either be together or don't, but carrying on between Eagles Nest and Boston makes no sense to me. What happened with your appointment?"

"He wants me to keep track of everything I sell for the rest of the week."

"You don't normally?"

"I haven't been. I figured all that mattered was what we made at the end of the day."

"But if you don't know how much inventory it took to get there..."

Abigail sighed. "Exactly. Luke is right about that." And great to look at. "I just need to develop some new habits."

"Never a fun process."

"Nope. The thing is, I tend to concentrate on what I like doing—the baking—and forget the stuff I don't—like paperwork."

"Ugh, paperwork. I'd rather create ten designs than spend an hour entering data on a spreadsheet, but it's gotta be done."

Spreadsheet. Now there was a word to strike terror into her heart. She'd never met one she hadn't loathed on sight, but evidently Roxanne was on speaking terms with the beast. Instead of admitting her aversion to her friend, she nodded. "Absolutely."

Embarrassment had kept her from confiding her financial problems to either

Roxanne or Ingrid, although Ingrid might suspect something wasn't quite right. "Luke has a good grasp of how to run a business. I'm going to do my best to follow his recommendations." If he'd create spreadsheets for her, she'd supply him with cookies for life.

"Is he cute?"

Abigail smiled, happy to focus on Luke instead of her sorry finances. "Yes."

"That helps."

"Hey, you guys!" Ingrid came through the open door. "I brought the one-and-a-half-liter bottle of wine this time."

"Party, party!" Roxanne grinned. "Set it on the coffee table, girlfriend. I'll get the opener and the glasses." She hurried into her small kitchen.

Ingrid glanced at Abigail. "How did it go?"

"He wants us to keep track of everything we sell for the next four days. He needs data."

"Probably a good idea. Did he flirt with you? Ask you out?"

"No, he did not."

"Well, damn. Did you flirt?"

"No! This is about business."

"What is?" Roxanne came back and started uncorking the wine.

"My meeting with Luke today. Ingrid's trying to turn it into a hot date."

"Well, you said he was cute." Roxanne pulled the cork out with a loud pop.

"Is that all she said?" Ingrid rolled her eyes. "She didn't mention the pecs, the abs or the ass on that cowboy?"

"A cowboy?" Roxanne poured wine into three glasses. "You didn't say anything about that, girl."

"Clearly you didn't give Roxanne all the pertinent facts." Ingrid picked up two glasses and handed one to Abigail.

"I didn't think it was import—"

"It's always important," Roxanne said. "I was picturing him in a boring shirt and tie."

"Hell, no." Ingrid glanced at Roxanne. "He strolled in wearing boots, snug jeans, a sheepskin jacket and a Stetson. Six-feet-three inches of muscled yumminess."

"If I'd known that, I'd have taken a break to wander down there. No wonder you're not upset about having to count all those pastries."

Abigail's cheeks warmed. "It's strictly business."

"If you say so." Roxanne raised her glass. "Here's to mixing business with pleasure." She winked at Abigail. "And if you haven't considered it, you wouldn't be blushing."

* * *

Besides retrieving the dog and saying hello to his Appaloosa, Spot On, Luke had arranged to meet Badger, Ryker and Trevor at the ranch. They'd all agreed to help him renovate his house, although Badger had admitted he'd never so much as used a hammer before.

Luke had invited them over for pizza and beer so they could see the place and brainstorm ideas for remodeling it. They'd decided to meet at the barn and go over together.

For someone who'd only been in town a couple of weeks, he'd made rapid progress toward his goals. He could thank Badger, who'd likely be his brother-in-law eventually. Over Christmas Badger and Luke's sister Hayley had engineered a fake engagement and now were together for real.

Hayley was still wrapping up her obligations in Denver and hadn't moved to Eagles Nest yet. Badger had, though, and was now a full partner in Badger Air, a commuter airline started by Ryker McGavin.

That friendship between Ryker and Badger, forged when they were both fighter pilots in the Air Force, had provided Luke with a connection to the McGavin family. Because of it he'd had the inside track on a five-acre property adjacent to Wild Creek Ranch.

The house had stood vacant for a couple of years while the heirs had debated whether to sell or renovate. Luke's offer of cash had convinced them to let it go.

Being neighbors with the McGavins had come with benefits. Kendra had advised him on the purchase of his Appaloosa and was giving him a good deal on boarding. She'd stabled the gelding in the old barn as if knowing Luke would enjoy having Spot On mixed in with the family's horses. Clearly she considered Luke one of them, now, an honorary McGavin. That touched him.

Badger's truck was already parked near the barn, so Luke drove through a patch of slush and pulled in next to it. The guy had insisted on a red one. The only child of wealthy parents in Atlanta, he'd owned several sports cars. Although he'd rejected that life when he'd enlisted, he still liked to make a splash now and then.

Luke's truck was beige. He'd bought a dark blue vintage pickup in high school and he'd scoured the internet until he'd found one almost like it except for the color. He and Faith, Cody McGavin's sweetheart, had bonded on the subject of classic trucks. She had one, too.

Everywhere he turned, the evidence was mounting that he'd made the right decision by leaving his urban life in Portland. Although he'd never lived in Eagles Nest, it felt like home.

A warm barn on a winter's night was one of the coziest places he knew. When he walked in and slid the door shut, the fragrance of hay and horses greeted him, along with the dog he'd rescued. She'd been hanging out with Badger at the far end of the barn, but she made a beeline for Luke once she spotted him.

He crouched down to give her a hug and a rub behind the ears. "How're you doing, pup? Been enjoying ranch life?"

"Kendra's convinced she was a ranch dog." Badger approached, his pace leisurely as always. "I showed up at feedin' time, and she was down here with the dog, who seemed to be right at home."

"Is that true, girl?" He gazed into the pup's golden eyes. "Did you live on a ranch?"

The dog stared at him, her brow wrinkled.

"If only she could talk," Badger said.

"She damn near can. Just now I got a definite yes from her." Luke stood. "Is Kendra up at the house?"

"Yep. She got a call regardin' a trail ride booking and had to go check somethin' on the computer. I asked her to leave the dog with me. I like dogs."

"Ever have one?"

"No." Badger leaned down and ruffled the pup's ears. "I was shipped off to school pretty early on. I wouldn't mind havin' one if Hayley's okay with it. And a couple of horses once we get settled."

"She should like all that. What do you hear from her?"

"She's plannin' on comin' over in about ten days. Might stay a week this time."

"Great. It'll be good to see her. And speaking of horses, I'm gonna pay a visit to mine, if you'd like to walk down there with me."

"I wouldn't mind." Badger fell into step beside him. The pup followed close behind.

"I appreciate that you signed on for this remodeling project."

"Don't thank me yet. Southern boys in my neighborhood didn't build treehouses and such. If we wanted one, our folks hired an architect."

Luke grinned. "You're making that up."

"I'm not sayin' I had a fancified one, but a kid down the block did. It was a lousy treehouse, too. A bunch of weird angles and a motorized ladder that didn't work right."

"Then you've never hammered a nail into a board just for the hell of it?"

"It's not like my father had a workbench and tools. Although now I wish I had more experience so I'd be of better use to your renovation team. I can't wait to see the place."

"Meant to get you over there sooner."

"No worries. You've been in there what— a week?"

"About that." Luke paused next to the Appaloosa's stall. "Hey, boy."

The gelding's ears flicked in recognition but he was busy with his dinner. Luke had hoped to arrive in time to help feed, but his appointment with Abigail had kept him in town longer than he'd anticipated.

"They aren't much for talkin' when they're eatin'." Badger leaned against the door and watched Spot On munching on a flake of hay.

"I've noticed."

"That's a handsome animal you have there. I'm partial to Paints since meetin' Winston down yonder." He tipped his head toward the far end of the barn. "But I can see the appeal of an Appaloosa. No two look alike."

"I know. I promised myself if I ever got a horse of my own, this is what I'd want." He glanced at Badger. "Any estimates on when Hayley will move here?"

"She's shootin' for sometime next month, but she's not plannin' to live with me once she moves here. At least not at first. She thinks we need more time to get to know each other."

"That sounds like her."

"I'm not pushing. I mucked it up before and I don't want to do it again."

.on't. She's crazy about you. But I
.mmendation if you want to hear it."

"I surely do. I need all the help I can get."

"Don't start suggesting things the minute she gets here. Wait a bit and she if she comes up with a plan."

"Thanks, Luke. Appreciate it."

About that time the barn door slid open and Ryker and Trevor came in. The dog hesitated only a moment before trotting over to accept some attention from both men.

"Nice dog you have," Ryker said.

"Not my dog."

"So you say. Are we having a pizza and beer party or what?"

"That's exactly what we're having." He shook hands with Ryker and Trevor. "I've already ordered it and we need to get over to my place so we're there when it's delivered."

"Can I come?" Kendra walked into the barn behind them. Slim and athletic, she didn't look like she could be the mother of five grown boys.

All the guys, including Luke, assured her that she was more than welcome.

"That's okay." She laughed. "I was just kidding. It's nice to be wanted, but Faith and Cody are coming over tonight to sort through the stuff in his closet. They've promised to take what they want and pack up the rest for Goodwill."

Ryker snorted. "The rest of us did that years ago."

"I know, but Cody's—"

"*The baby*!" Ryker and Trevor chorused. They both rolled their eyes.

Folding her arms, Kendra gazed at them with amused tolerance. "Somebody had to be. Aren't you glad it was him and not either of you?"

Ryker and Trevor exchanged glances. Ryker nodded. "Yes, ma'am, I'm very glad."

"Me, too," Trevor said. "Despite the fact he was spoiled rotten."

"Enough of that." Ryker angled his head toward the front of the barn. "We need to make tracks."

"Yeah, we do, but I have something for your mom. Be right back." He told the pup to stay and she did. Someone had trained her well. He hurried out to the truck and grabbed the brownies.

Kendra was thrilled with them. "They're my favorite snack. I'll give her a call tomorrow."

"If you make it around two in the afternoon, she'll probably have time to talk."

"Then I'll do that."

"And thank you so much for watching the pup." He stroked the dog's head.

"Anytime."

"Guess we'll be off, then." He touched the brim of his hat in farewell before raising his voice. "Okay, everybody follow me."

The other three gave Kendra a hug before leaving the barn.

A few minutes later, with the dog sitting alert and quivering in the passenger seat, he led the caravan of pickups over to his place. *His place.* He sure loved thinking of it that way.

The house was dark because he hadn't bought timers for the lamps yet. He'd do that soon because he liked the visual of a light shining in the window, welcoming him home.

The dog whined as he parked and turned off the engine. She did that every time they came back here, as if she couldn't wait to get inside.

"Hang on, girl." Taking her leash out of the console, he walked around to the passenger side and opened the door. "Stay, pup."

She trembled with eagerness but didn't move as he clipped the leash to her collar. He used it to make sure she didn't take a notion to run into the woods after some critter. Maybe she wouldn't, but he wasn't taking that chance. She'd ended up on that highway somehow. He picked up the box of cookies from the floor and opened the door wider. "Okay, girl. You can get out."

She hopped down and walked beside him across the snow-packed ground. What a good dog she was. He couldn't believe nobody had come looking for her.

The guys piled out of their trucks as Luke climbed the steps, unlocked the front door and flicked on the lights. He led the dog inside and took off her leash. She headed for the kitchen, clearly ready for dinner.

"In a minute, girl."

The guys came in raving about his cool hideaway in the pines. The dog reappeared and began to mingle, greeting everybody and allowing herself to be petted.

"It's like this pup is the welcome committee." Badger rubbed behind her ears. "Did you train her to do that?"

"Hardly. You're the first company I've had since I found her. She must have done that in her other life." He smiled as the dog moved on to Ryker.

He crouched down to pet her. "Guess it's my turn." He glanced at Luke. "You lucked out on this house, buddy. Knotty pine. Nice."

"The whole house is paneled in it. Definite selling point for me."

"It's the good stuff, too." Trevor walked over to run his hand down the nearest wall.

"Neither of you've been in this house?"

Ryker shook his head. "I haven't. Trev, did you ever come over here?"

"Nope. I doubt any of us did. I think Mom tried to strike up a friendship with the couple, since they were neighbors and all. But nothing came of it. Happens sometimes."

Badger surveyed the room. "Great place, though. Makes me think of an old-timey cabin, one you'd rent for the summer."

"I like it, too," Trevor said. "The fireplace is awesome. Have you had a fire in it, yet?"

"Several. I bought it partly for the fireplace. It's all set to go for tonight's brainstorming session."

"Speaking of that," Ryker said, "we need a tour."

"You bet. Won't take long." He started toward the hall. "Two bedrooms, master bath, laundry room, and storage closets down this way."

The dog abandoned Ryker and trotted ahead of Luke.

"Looks like your pup wants to show us her house," Badger said.

"Yeah, she acts like she owns the place," Trevor said, laughing.

She did, at that. As Luke took everyone through the first bedroom, which he'd set up as an office, the dog stood in the middle of the crowd wagging her tail and grinning as if to say *isn't this great?*

She repeated the routine in the master bedroom and even nudged her dog bed as if wanting to show it off. *Good luck keeping your distance.* Abigail's words came back to him.

While the guys inspected the dining room and the kitchen, Trevor started making notes on his phone. Luke grabbed the opportunity to give the dog her dinner and demonstrate her strange habit of only eating on command.

Ryker shook his head. "I've never seen a dog do that before. The ones we had growing up would charge that bowl."

"Yep," Trevor said. "That's one unusual animal you have there, Luke."

"I don't know that much about dogs, but I guess she has some quirks."

"She's smart, too," Ryker said. "That's the border collie in her." He glanced at Luke. "How come you haven't given her a name?"

"Because it wouldn't be the name she's used to and it might confuse her."

"I doubt it. Animals get used to being called several names. Besides, if she ends up being your dog, you'll need a name then."

"I know, but—"

"Your call. But she has so much personality and...it seems weird to just call her *girl* and *pup* all the time."

It was weird. But once he named her, letting her go would be that much harder. Which meant *not* naming her was his issue, not hers. She deserved a name, even a temporary one.

He took a deep breath. "Okay, you're right. She needs a name, but what? I haven't thought about—" The doorbell rang. "Pizza's here." He walked into the living room.

"Perfect timing." Ryker followed him. "We'll figure out the dog's name while we're eating."

Luke glanced over his shoulder. "Aren't we supposed to be brainstorming the renovations?"

"We can do that, too. We'll multitask."

Two hours later, they'd discussed upgrading the dated bathroom and potentially knocking out the wall between the two bedrooms to create a master suite. The knotty pine would stay and the carpet would go. Trevor used a pocket knife to rip up a corner of it in the living room and discovered hardwood flooring underneath.

Replacing windows might have to wait until spring. Trevor recommended refinishing the kitchen cabinets and tiling the kitchen floor. They all agreed on replacing the overhead light in the

. with a rustic chandelier they found

But they couldn't agree on a name for the
several were proposed and shot down.

Badger studied the dog lying on a rug in
front of the fireplace gnawing on a chew toy. "Or
we can just call her Delilah."

"Delilah?" Luke stared at him. "Why
would we call her that?"

"It was my great-aunt's name. I loved that
woman. Smart, independent, and feisty as hell."

Ryker took a sip of his beer. "It certainly
has a ring to it."

"It does," Trevor said. "I've never known a
dog with that name. It's unusual."

"And so is she. I like it, too." Luke glanced
around. "Everybody in favor?"

They all nodded.

"Then Delilah it is." He lifted his beer
bottle. "To Delilah."

Her head came up and her tail thumped
the floor.

"To Delilah!" the guys echoed.

She looked straight at Luke as if she knew
something important had happened.

"Hey, Delilah," he murmured.

She got up and came to him, eyes bright,
tail wagging.

The stakes had gone up. If someone
claimed her, he wouldn't be giving up a dog he'd
rescued. He'd be giving up Delilah.

5

Abigail had done it, by God. She had numbers for Luke, impressive numbers. Even she was surprised by the volume of inventory that had gone out the door in the past four days. She stapled the sheaf of papers together and laid them on the counter. He should arrive any minute.

The bell on the front door jangled but it was Roxanne, not Luke. She'd worn a jacket but hadn't bothered to zip it since she'd only had to brave the cold the short distance from the apartments' entrance door to this one. "He's due at four, right?"

"Right."

"Figured I'd find out if you have any leftovers and time it so I might see this guy who's got you doing math. I want to make sure he's good enough for you."

"For the last time, I'm not dating him." Ever since Wednesday night, Abigail had been dealing with Ingrid's and Roxanne's matchmaking fantasies. Both thought Luke sounded like boyfriend material, someone who could coax her out of the celibate life she'd been leading ever since moving to Eagles Nest.

"You may not be dating him *now.* But you could be dating him very soon if you play your cards right."

"I'm not playing any cards. I'm only trying to get a better handle on my business so I can make it more efficient." And profitable.

"I'm willing to believe that's your motivation. He, on the other hand, might be thinking you're really hot."

"Stop it, Roxanne."

"All right. Changing subjects. Is everything left in the case up for grabs? And are you available for another movie night after you finish up with Luke?"

"It is and I am. I can sleep in tomorrow."

"Yay. But if Mister Gorgeous asks you out, you can ditch us. We won't be offended."

"He won't ask me out."

"You never know."

"I'll get you a box."

"Thanks." She walked around behind the case and peered in. "There's a lot still in here. Are you sure you want me to take it all?"

"Sure. In fact, you'll need two boxes."

"Yeah, I will. You and Ingrid baked up a storm today."

"It was wall-to-wall customers at one, so Ingrid stayed a little late to put a few more batches in the oven. I thought the rush might keep up but it didn't." Abigail handed her the first box and fit the tabs in the slots of the second one. "Are you guys really planning to eat all this?"

"Oh, hell, no." Roxanne took the second box, filled it and set it on the counter. "If we ate everything you gave us, we'd balloon up in no time."

"So you throw it away?"

"Nope. We choose our favorites and the rest goes to the Eagles Nest Food Bank."

"No kidding? That's awesome!"

"Evidently that old guy who used to rent my apartment did it and Ingrid followed suit. I'm just keeping up the tradition. Ingrid and I take turns running it over there."

"What a terrific idea. I can't believe I didn't think of it."

"You have plenty going on without adding a trip to the food bank. We're happy to be the delivery service."

"I'm thrilled that you and Ingrid are doing it. Thanks."

"You're so welcome. I—" The front door opened and she turned. Without missing a beat, she rounded the counter and held out her hand. "You must be Luke. I'm Roxanne. I live upstairs."

He took off his Stetson and shook her hand. "Nice to meet you, ma'am. I like your artwork on the window. Great job." He laid his laptop case on the nearest table.

"Thank you. That's kind of you to say."

"Abigail mentioned you're a graphic designer." He unbuttoned his jacket.

Abigail's breath caught as he shrugged out of it and hung it over the back of a chair. He was even sexier than she'd remembered.

"Yep. At your service." Roxanne acted nonchalant.

Abigail wasn't fooled. Roxanne was enjoying the heck out of this encounter.

"Would that include creating website headers and logos?"

"Absolutely. My cards are upstairs, but—"

"No worries," Abigail said. "I'll make sure he has your number and email."

"Great. Thanks. I'll get out of here so you two can talk." As she walked to the counter and picked up the bakery boxes, she gave Abigail a subtle thumbs-up. "Nice meeting you, Luke." She headed for the door.

"Same here, Roxanne," he called after her. Then he turned to Abigail and smiled. "How've you been?"

"Busy." His smile played havoc with her poise. "Busy counting."

"That's great! Then you have some data for me?"

"I do." She snatched up the pages and came around the counter. "Here you go. Scads of data."

He glanced over the first page and flipped to the second. "Excellent. Can I keep these?"

"Of course. Can I get you some coffee?" She hadn't made him cookies this time. Hadn't wanted to overdo it. "I'd offer you a pastry but Roxanne took them all."

"I don't need coffee right now, thanks. And no problem about the pastries, either. But they're in the count for today, right?"

"Yes. Listed as unsold leftovers."

"Must have been quite a few if she needed two boxes to carry them all." He flipped to the back of the list. "Ah, here they are. That's a lot of excess inventory."

"We overbaked today more than usual. I was fooled into thinking the early afternoon rush would last."

"Hm." He gestured toward the chair where he'd left his coat. "Let's sit."

"Okay." Adorable as he was to look at, that speculative *hm* made her nervous. "I hate to run out of stuff."

"I get that." He waited until she was seated before taking the opposite chair. "But if it causes you to bake more than you can sell, that's costing you money."

"But a big chunk of the extra goes to the food bank."

His eyebrows rose. "It does? Are you documenting that for tax purposes?"

"Well...no."

"That would be helpful."

"I will from now on."

"Good, but I have a recommendation."

"All right." She braced herself.

"Take everything that's left over and sell it at a discount the next day. I realize that won't work on Saturdays, but—"

"You want me to sell stale baked goods?" The idea horrified her.

"I doubt they're stale if you baked them later in the day because you were running low."

"I know, but I'm *labeling* them stale! What will the sign say? *Day-old baked goods.* That's code for stale."

"I don't see it that way. And you—"

about the food bank? I'd be taking
m the mouths of disadvantaged

"You could donate whatever doesn't sell
if you put it out the second time."

"That's not very nice. Then they get
leftover leftovers."

"Yes, it is. It's very nice. It's free food." His
gaze was kind as it met hers. "I'm sure you could
wrap everything up well so it stayed fresh."

"You're killing me with these suggestions,
Luke."

"You said the money would soon run out.
I'm trying to put my finger in the dike."

She sighed. "Day-old baked goods will
ruin my reputation."

"No, it won't."

"I've built my business on that right-out-
of-the-oven smell. Day-old pastries don't smell like
that."

"But they'll be cheaper. Some folks who
couldn't buy them at full price could afford them
at half-price."

She slumped in her chair. "That's a
thought. I'll cling to it. Anything else? Or is that my
assignment for the week?"

"I do have another recommendation."

She cringed. "I'm afraid to hear what it is."

"Raise your prices."

"*What?*" She slapped the table with both
hands. "That's crazy! Customers will complain. I'll
lose business. Absolutely not. I won't do it."

"Five percent. That's not a huge raise."

"Any raise is huge. Pastries are a luxury item. Raise the price and customers decide they don't need that cheese Danish, after all. I've seen it happen."

"Really?"

"Maybe not, but I've seen it in my nightmares. I'm not doing it, Luke. Everything I've built so far will melt away."

"I disagree. You're underpriced."

She glared at him. "I like giving folks a bargain."

"You want to be known as a bargain bakery?"

"Of course not, but—"

"If you undervalue your product, eventually people will think it must be inferior."

"I don't believe that."

"Believe it. You've only been in business for a year, but if you keep prices this low eventually customers will decide that what you offer must be mediocre. Otherwise you'd charge more."

"No, they wouldn't think that."

"Let's test it. Raise your prices next week. If you get a flood of complaints and business is terrible, you can always switch back to the way it was. Hang onto the old price labels just in case."

"But if customers get upset—"

"They might buy the day-old items and get their baked goods even cheaper. They could be thrilled with this new plan."

"Or they might leave and never come back."

"You're the only bakery in town. They'll come back." He paused. "You've admitted things have to change. Give people credit for being willing to pay for superior baked goods like yours."

"It'll be a disaster, a week of pain and suffering."

"Maybe not. If it is, we'll adjust. I'll drop by on Friday afternoon and see how you're doing. Be sure and keep all the receipts and we'll do a profit and loss statement for those five days. If it's a disaster, I'll help you put the old prices back up."

"What if it's too late? What if I've ticked off all my customers and turned my bakery into an empty shell of a business?"

Luke favored her with another smile. "That isn't going to happen."

"Easy for you to say."

"Want to bag the program?"

She did, but unless she changed her methods, Pie in the Sky would fail. That wouldn't feel so damn good, either. She'd sunk her inheritance into this business, all her parents' hard-earned money. If that money went down the drain, she'd never forgive herself.

Dragging in a breath, she looked at the tall cowboy sitting in the too-small chair. "I don't want to bag the program. I want to save my business. But damn, these solutions are depressing."

"I can see that. Tell you what. Let me take you to dinner at the GG. I don't know any place more likely to cheer up a person than the GG."

"You're asking me out?" She hadn't anticipated this development. But Roxanne had.

"Yes. I don't want to leave here with you looking so sad."

"So this is a pity date?"

"No!" He cleared his throat. "I'd very much like to take you to dinner. I hope you'll agree to go."

Her brain was whirling with excitement but she wasn't so completely distracted that she forgot one important fact. "What about the dog? Do you still have her?"

"The *dog.* Yes, and thanks for reminding me. Kendra's watching her. I'll find out if she can stay at the ranch a little longer." He stood. "My phone's in my jacket."

He left the table, which gave Abigail a chance to collect herself. He'd asked her out, but not necessarily because he thought she was hot. Judging from what he'd said, he might be feeling sorry for her.

She could choose to reject the offer. On the other hand, she hadn't had dinner with a handsome man in a very long time. She'd accept.

Tucking his phone away, he came back to the table. "Kendra's willing to keep Delilah for the rest of the evening."

"Delilah? I thought you weren't going to name her."

"I wasn't. It's a long story. I'll tell you at dinner." Vulnerability flickered for an instant in his eyes. "That's if you want to go."

"I'd love to."

"Good." He looked relieved. "Is there anything you need to do before we take off?"

"One phone call."

"Sure thing."

"Be right back." She retrieved her phone from behind the counter and walked into her office before calling Roxanne. "He asked me out," she murmured.

The response was so loud, excited and inappropriate that she laughed and hung up.

Roxanne texted her immediately. *Told you so.*

6

Almost screwed that up. Luke wasn't proud of the way he'd bobbled the dinner invite, but at least Abigail had agreed to go with him despite his dumb remark about not wanting to leave her feeling sad.

After he'd helped her into the cab of his truck and climbed behind the wheel, he breathed in the aroma of cookies baking. She'd brought that tempting scent with her. Talk about an aphrodisiac.

"This is a great truck." She ran her hand over the dash. "Did you restore it?"

"Wish I could say I did." He rested his arm on the back of the bench seat and shifted into reverse. He sure was enjoying being close to this sweet-smelling woman. "I bought it this way. I figured renovating my house would keep me busy without trying to restore a truck at the same time."

"You're renovating a house?"

"Not by myself." He waited for traffic to clear and backed out. "Three guys are helping me."

"Sounds like fun."

"I'm sure it will be. I've never owned a house. I can't wait to see how it turns out."

"I guess you could say I've owned a house. I inherited the one my folks had. But it didn't feel like mine."

"I can see how it wouldn't." He wanted to reach over and give her hand a reassuring squeeze. But despite this dinner date, they were still only business associates.

He settled for talking instead of touching her. "I can't imagine what that must have been like, handling it all by yourself."

"It wasn't a walk in the park. But I survived it and here I am." She gave him a smile.

"And I'm glad you are."

"When you worked for the restaurant chain in Portland, did you get them to raise their prices?"

"Yes, ma'am."

"And it worked out?"

"Sure did. They wanted to promote themselves as upscale, but their prices were midrange. We raised the prices and business got better."

"But that's Portland."

"No, that's people. They tell you they want a bargain, and they do, but then they question whether the product can be top quality if it's so cheap."

"That's not fair."

"Maybe not, but we all do it. Think of the last thing you got at a really low price."

She unzipped her jacket. "This sweater. It was half-price."

"Looks pretty on you." He'd admired how the sage green brought out the green in her eyes.

"I love the color and it's a good brand, but..." She laughed. "I examined the seams and decided it might be a knockoff. So instead of saving it for special occasions I wear it for work."

"See? Bet you wouldn't be examining seams if you'd paid full price."

"No, and I wouldn't be wearing it to bake in. You've made your point. But I still dread raising prices. My customers are my friends."

"Friends would want you to stay in business." He pulled into the GG parking lot. "But speaking of that, what do you say we don't talk about business any more tonight?"

"Great idea."

"Now all we need is a parking spot. The place is jammed."

"There's one."

"So there is." He grabbed it and switched off the engine. "Stay put, okay? There's a puddle on your side."

"I'll be fine. I'm wearing boots."

"That may be the case." He took his hat from the dash and settled it on his head. "But when I ask a lady to dinner, I don't expect her to wade through puddles." He got out and rounded the truck.

She had a small lake on her side. Opening the door, he straddled the puddle and held out his arms. "Fair damsel, allow me to lift you over this large and very dangerous body of water. No telling what's in there. Barracuda, maybe."

"Then I'm lucky you're here to save me." She clutched his shoulders.

"Here we go." He grabbed hold of her and swung her over to a dry spot. Then it was time to let go, but he didn't want to.

"My hero." She gazed up at him, a smile in her eyes and her hands still resting on his jacket.

She was flirting with him. Good sign. "Glad to be of service, ma'am." He exaggerated the drawl. "If there's ever anything you need, just—"

"Hey, Luke!"

So much for that moment. Luke let go of Abigail and turned. Trevor and the dark-haired woman he was in love with crossed the parking lot, dodging puddles.

Luke had spaced the woman's name. He'd met her at the Christmas talent show. She was an accountant and her name was...

"Hi, Abigail!" Trevor smiled. "Olivia and I were going in to grab a bite and maybe dance a little. Would you two like to join us?"

Olivia. That was it.

"Love to," Abigail said.

"Sure, why not?" Luke added. "Nice to see you again, Olivia."

"Same here, Luke. I heard you bought a house."

"Sure did. Trevor's going to be a big help getting it in shape."

"Trevor's one of your three guys?" Abigail looked delighted with the info.

"I am," Trevor said. "Ryker and Badger are my helpers."

"Then you're in good hands, Luke." Abigail smiled at him. "Your house will be awesome."

"Guaranteed. Hey, I vote we head inside. It's cold out here."

"Good idea." Abigail ended up walking in with Olivia and chatting with her.

Which was fine. But if he'd planned on a cozy dinner for two, that scenario was down the drain. Then again, this might be better, more low-key so he and Abigail could gradually get to know each other.

Trevor had mentioned dancing, though. Abigail might dance and she might not, but if she did, that could serve as an icebreaker. Live music greeted them as they walked in so the band was already playing.

Michael was behind the bar and Luke gave him a wave. This had been a good idea. Saturday night at the GG was one of the reasons to live in Eagles Nest. Good food and live music were hard to beat. Maybe tonight Bryce and Nicole would perform a few numbers. They'd been awesome at the talent show.

He hadn't managed to get to the GG for dinner since moving to Eagles Nest, but he'd do better from now on. No point in living here if he didn't enjoy what the town had to offer.

They scored the last table next to the dance floor. Luke wasn't surprised. Trevor was Bryce's twin and probably rated preferential treatment at the GG.

After everyone had hung their coats over their chairs and ordered, Trevor turned to Luke. "What's up with Delilah?"

"She's fine. She's out at the ranch with your mom."

"I'm sure Mom's loving that."

"I hope so."

"Count on it. She loves animals, and a hard-luck case like Delilah would be right up her alley. How's that pup doing?"

"Great. I could probably leave her alone when I have appointments, but after what she's been through, I sort of hate to. I take her with me when I can."

"Then bring her with you to the bakery next time," Abigail said.

"You wouldn't mind?"

"Of course I wouldn't. I'd love to see how she's doing. I'd have one of my own except it's not fair to keep a dog cooped up in an apartment while I work all day."

"Then that's a deal."

"Hey, guys," Trevor said. "Since our food's not here yet, who's ready to dance?"

Luke glanced at Abigail. "Want to?"

Her smile told him the answer before she said the words. "Love to."

"Then let's do it." His heart pumped faster as he led her out on the floor. The dance was a quick two-step, not a romantic waltz. But he'd take it.

Her eyes sparkled as he led her through the intricate steps and the brief but sizzling moments when he held her close heated his blood. They were both breathing hard when the dance ended.

And she was grinning. "That was a blast."

"Uh-huh. I'm glad I remembered how."

"You didn't dance in Portland?"

"Not country. It's there, but I wasn't in that crowd." He was ready to keep going but a glance at the table told him the food had arrived. "Time to eat." He wrapped his arm around her waist on the way back to the table. Felt like the natural thing to do.

"You two looked good out there," Olivia said.

"I love the two-step." Abigail settled her napkin in her lap. "Luke's a great partner." She met his gaze. "What did you mean that you weren't *in that crowd* in Portland?"

"I got into the whole urban professional role. I thought that was how I had to package myself to succeed."

Trevor shook his head. "That sounds messed up."

"It was. Took me a few years to figure out what I wanted, though."

"Us," Trevor said with a chuckle. "You wanted us."

"Exactly. Small town, people who wouldn't flinch if I showed up for an appointment looking like a cowboy."

Trevor put down his beer mug. "Around here, folks prefer that."

"I certainly do," Abigail said. Then she blushed. "I mean, it's more in keeping with the town's spirit and all."

"Definitely." Trevor glanced at her and back at Luke with a knowing smile. "Goes with the ambiance."

Luke savored the meaning of that blush for the rest of the meal. She liked him. Evidently she also liked that he was a cowboy at heart. He didn't ride the range, but he had a classic pickup, a horse and a dog. A herding dog, at that.

During the meal, Trevor wanted to talk about Luke's house and Abigail seemed curious about it. That was fine, too. He'd like to take her out there some time.

When the plates were cleared away, Trevor announced he was ready for more dancing. Luke offered his hand to Abigail and she took it with a smile.

But it wasn't a two-step this time. As the gentle rhythm of a waltz flowed around them, Luke drew Abigail close while holding her gaze. She didn't look away.

The silent communication of their bodies fired his imagination. She still smelled like cookies and he wanted to bury his nose in her fragrant hair. He wouldn't, though. If he moved too fast with this woman, he'd regret it.

They hadn't even kissed.

Oh, but he wanted to kiss her. Her full mouth tempted him, especially at moments like this, when her eyes glowed with happiness.

When the song ended, he was still captured by the warmth of her gaze.

"This has been lovely," she murmured.

"Sure has." His earlier decision about taking it slow began to dissolve in the intensity arcing between them.

"But...I've been up since three this morning."

Yikes. He'd totally forgotten about that. "Say no more. I'll take you home."

"I feel like a party pooper."

"You're not. The rest of us don't keep your hours. You've had a much longer day than we have."

"The perils of being a baker."

"It's a worthy sacrifice. You make folks real happy." He hooked his arm around her waist again. "Let's say our goodbyes."

They left Trevor and Olivia with promises to get together again soon. The puddle beside the truck had frozen, so Luke just had to make sure Abigail didn't slip and fall. Not as much fun as swinging her over the puddle.

Once they were on their way, she leaned her head against the seat with a happy sigh. "What a wonderful evening. Thank you for inviting me."

"You're welcome. Maybe we could do it again sometime." His chest tightened.

"I'd like that."

What a relief. "Me, too."

"But I'm not clear on this mixing business with pleasure thing. Is seeing each other socially going to interfere with our business relationship?"

He had an answer for that one. "When I take on a client, I want the best for them, always. Your success with Pie in the Sky takes priority. I won't let anything interfere with that."

"Well, then. That gives us plenty of leeway, doesn't it?"

"I think so." He parked in front of her apartment entrance. "I'll help you out."

"No." She laid a hand on his arm. "Let me go in by myself. If you come to the door, we'll probably want to kiss goodnight and I'm not quite ready for that." She smiled. "And I'd like to be more alert when it happens."

He blew out a breath. "Okay."

"Goodnight, Luke. Thank you."

"It was my pleasure. See you Friday afternoon." He watched as she walked to the door. Before going in, she turned and waved. He flashed the headlights.

Then he drove away and ignored the ache of longing coursing through him. He hadn't exactly *counted* on a goodnight kiss. Well, yeah, maybe he had. But he admired her reasoning. A first kiss should be special, and she was holding out for special.

That put her decision to walk herself to the door in a whole new light. A very promising light. But damn, he wasn't supposed to see her for another week.

Maybe he'd stop by Tuesday or Wednesday and find out how she was doing. But was that a good idea? She'd be testing his recommendations and it might be best for her if he stayed away and let that play out.

On the other hand, maybe paying her a visit would be a way of giving her valuable moral support. He didn't know anymore, which meant he was letting personal feelings interfere with his professional judgment. He'd promised her that wouldn't happen. Time to get his head back in the game.

7

It was only their first date, and Abigail missed him already. She missed the warmth of his arms, the light in his eyes, the sound of his laughter. What a great evening.

Yet she hadn't been kidding about being tired. She wished he could be here right now to carry her up the stairs.

Not that she'd expect him to do that, but it was a fun fantasy. The masterful way he'd lifted her over the puddle had made an impression. He might have a white-collar job, but he had blue-collar muscles.

As she neared the top step, the hinges on a door down the hall gave a rusty creak. She started laughing. "Are you two spying on me?"

"Would that be a bad thing?" Roxanne opened her door and there she and Ingrid stood in their PJs, grinning at her.

"Not necessarily, but if you don't want me to catch you doing it, you'd better squirt some WD-40 on those hinges."

"Thanks for the tip." Roxanne walked into the hallway. "Are you too tired to come in for a minute?"

"Well, I—"

"Never mind," Ingrid said. "We'll talk tomorrow. Get some sleep."

But they'd been waiting and listening for her to get home. Like her mom used to. "I'll come in for a little while."

"We won't keep you long." Ingrid swung the door wide. "But we have treats."

"I know. We baked them."

"Not those treats. Roxanne and I opened the ginormous box of dark chocolate truffles she's been saving in the fridge since New Year's." Ingrid grabbed a gold box from the coffee table and held it out. "Have one."

Abigail plucked a truffle and bit into it. "Mm."

"Take another one," Roxanne said. "Chocolates are like champagne. Once you open them to the air, you need to finish them off."

Abigail popped the rest of the truffle into her mouth, picked out another one and took a seat on the floor beside the coffee table. "Thanks. Are these from an old boyfriend trying to get you back?"

"No, from my dad. He knows I love the good stuff."

"Props to him." She took a bite and talked around a mouthful of heaven. "They're amazing."

"So is my dad, but we're veering off topic and you baker ladies need your beauty sleep. Did you have a good time?"

"*Great* time. We went to the Guzzling Grizzly for dinner."

Ingrid smiled. "Nice. Did you dance?"

"Twice."

"Is he a good dancer?" Roxanne munched on another truffle. "I always count that a plus."

"Very good dancer. We managed a fast two-step without stepping on each other. And the slow dance was..." She paused. *Warm and sensual. Like something out of a movie.*

"Was what?" Ingrid prompted.

"Romantic. Seductive. But I was starting to fade. When I told him I was tired, he whisked me out of there and brought me straight home."

Ingrid sighed. "A true gentleman. Then what? A goodnight kiss?"

"He was ready to walk me to the door, but I asked him not to. When I kiss him for the first time, I don't want to be exhausted."

"Good call." Roxanne nodded. "It would be a shame to end a great evening with a mediocre lip-lock."

"I guess," Ingrid said. "It's just the classic ending to a first date."

"Unless you've been up since three in the morning." Roxanne put the lid on the box of chocolates. "Speaking of which, I move we adjourn."

"I second the motion." Abigail stood and grabbed her coat. "Thanks for the truffles."

"You're welcome." Roxanne got up and gave her a hug. "Thanks for the vicarious thrills. He seems like a great guy."

"I'm happy for you, girlfriend." Ingrid hugged her, too.

A rush of gratitude warmed her. She hadn't known either of these women very long, but they'd become a significant part of her world, almost like family. "Thanks for waiting up for me tonight, guys."

Roxanne smiled. "Then we don't have to get out the WD-40?"

"Nope. When I hear hinges squeaking, I'll know it's just you two watching out for me."

* * *

A little past ten on Sunday, Luke drove over to Wild Creek Ranch with Delilah riding shotgun. When he'd picked her up after his date with Abigail the night before, Kendra had assured him that the dog would be fine going with him when he took his Appaloosa out this morning. He was about to test it.

He looked forward to sucking up some of the crisp winter air. Maybe it would blow the cobwebs out of his brain. Concern about how he was handling the situation with Abigail had kept him from sleeping well.

Kendra walked out of the barn leading Spot On and carrying a grooming tote. Putting it down, she gave him a wave as he parked and shut off the engine.

She was every inch a cowgirl in her faded sheepskin jacket, worn jeans and boots, except for the red knit stocking cap she'd pulled over her dark hair. The splash of color stood out in a setting that was largely black, gray and white. Even his horse blended with the snowy landscape. Delilah, too, for that matter. He let her out and she trotted over to greet Kendra.

He followed, but evidently not fast enough to suit the dog. She returned, circled behind him and nudged him forward. He started laughing. "Is she herding me?"

"That's exactly what she's doing. She wants her peeps in a cluster rather than spread out." Kendra smiled as she watched the dog.

"That's funny. Okay, Delilah, I'm going." He lengthened his stride. When he reached the hitching post, the dog gave him a doggie grin of approval. "You're a hoot, girl." He scratched behind her ears.

"She was somebody's ranch dog. I just know it."

"If they live around here, they must not be trying very hard to find her." He glanced at Kendra. "I left my number and a description of Delilah with every shelter in the area and took out classified ads in the newspaper in both Bozeman and Billings. No one's shown up."

"That's crazy." She shoved her hands in her pockets. "Before she ended up on the highway *someone* was taking good care of her."

"And she's such a great dog. You'd think whoever lost her would be looking everywhere."

"Makes no sense. I'm just glad you found her."

"Me, too." But now that he had her, he wanted to make sure nothing bad happened to her. He was nervous about the ride today. "Are you positive I can just ride out of here and she'll trot along with me?"

"I am, but I'll keep her here if you want."

"No, I need to try this out. I'll make it a short ride, but I'll take her." He walked over to Spot On and Delilah followed. "Thanks for bringing my horse out."

"If you'd been ten minutes later I would have had him groomed for you."

He gave her a smile. "Thank you, but I'm not paying enough to get that kind of service."

"It's fun for me." She flipped her coat collar up against the chilly breeze. "Grooming an Appy is a visual treat and he's a sweetheart."

"Of course he is. You helped me choose him." He scratched the Appaloosa's silky neck and gave him the carrots in his jacket pocket.

"Well, he's turned out even better than I thought he would. And talk about visual treats, he and Delilah look perfect together, like you planned to get a black and white dog to go with your horse."

"I noticed they match up." Moving over to the tote, he took out a brush and began working on the gelding's coat.

"If you take Delilah out riding every time, they could become friends."

"I hadn't thought of that." He moved around to the horse's dappled rump. "But now that you mention it, I remember there was a dog at the stable where I used to ride as a kid. That dog clearly liked hanging out with the horses."

"Hey, watch Delilah. I think she's making an overture."

He paused and glanced at the dog.

She'd moved closer to Spot On. The gelding looked at the dog sitting in front of him and she gazed up at the horse, clearly expecting something. Slowly the Appaloosa lowered his head. They touched noses.

"Now that's cute."

"Like I said, they could easily become friends."

"Assuming someone doesn't come for Delilah in the next few days. It could happen."

"I know. I'll go fetch your tack."

"Kendra, I can—"

"It's no problem. I'm right here." She went into the barn.

That pretty much described Kendra in a nutshell. She was right there to lend a hand or dispense advice. Maybe she'd have some words of wisdom regarding Abigail.

He couldn't discuss her with his mom in case it might tempt her to stray off the path. Telling her about a potential woman in his life would be unfair if he didn't want her to swing into matchmaking mode. He'd considered calling Hayley in Denver but she didn't know Abigail. His dad would be more objective, but he really needed a woman's opinion.

She came back out with his tack and he thanked her. The custom made black saddle and the black bridle had been part of the deal she'd helped him find. Whenever she'd been involved, things had turned out well for him.

Still, this was a highly personal matter. He had to work up to it. He settled the blanket on the horse's back. "The GG was sure hopping last night."

"I'll bet. That band is excellent."

"It is." He lifted the saddle. "I had a great time. I think Abigail did, too. But..."

"But?" Kendra regarded him quietly as he positioned the saddle and tightened the cinch.

He could just say *never mind* and let the subject drop. She likely wouldn't ask him about it. "I'm attracted to her."

"That's not surprising. She's a lovely woman."

He paused and faced her. "She's fantastic. Generous, hard-working, kind. And she loves that bakery. Loves her work."

"You can see that the minute you walk in there."

"It's a great place. But if she doesn't turn things around, she'll lose it."

"Lose it?" Her eyes widened. "Why?"

"She hasn't managed her money very well."

"Oh, dear. What a shame."

"Yes, ma'am. She's been wearing blinders, partly from inexperience and partly because she'd rather bake than do paperwork."

"I get that. I'd rather muck out stalls than reconcile the accounts. I don't know anyone who likes paperwork, do you?"

"Me."

She chuckled. "Okay, I know one person. No, two. Olivia loves numbers."

"Not Abigail."

"Can you help her pull this out of the fire?"

"I can if she'll agree with my suggestions."

"And will she?"

"I sure hope so. But some will go against the grain. And if we're emotionally involved..."

"Hm." She frowned. "That puts you in a tough spot."

"Yes, ma'am."

"She could potentially reject your advice."

"She could."

"And you along with it."

His breath hitched. She'd put her finger on the pressure point, the tender source of his anxiety. "Guess so."

"That's a worst-case scenario." Her voice gentled. "It's also possible that everything will work out."

"But it might be better to keep my distance?"

Her gaze filled with compassion. "Only you can answer that, Luke."

8

All week Abigail braced for the worst, but it never came. If anyone noticed the higher prices, they didn't mention it. Sales were as brisk as ever. Most of the half-priced items sold, too.

When Luke arrived a little after four, he was not alone. He'd brought Delilah, just as she'd suggested. The dog had a snazzy red collar and a matching leash. She looked proud of both.

Luke seemed a little hesitant about bringing her in the shop, though. "Is this still okay?"

"Of course! Take off her leash so she can walk around. I'm sure she'll be fine." Abigail came around the counter. "Welcome to Pie in the Sky, Delilah."

Luke glanced at the empty bakery case. "Sold everything?"

"Most. Put the rest away to be discounted."

"Any problems? Complaints? Peasants with pitchforks?"

"Amazingly, no."

"Did business fall off?"

"No. In fact, it picked up."

He grinned as he unbuttoned his jacket. "Excellent."

"Is it okay if I get Delilah a bowl of water?"

"She'd love that." Luke set down his laptop case before unhooking Delilah's leash and tucking it in his coat pocket.

"But first let me make friends with this beautiful girl." She crouched in front of the dog and held out her hand, palm down. "How are you doing, Delilah? Has Luke been treating you well since the last time I saw you?"

Tail wagging, Delilah sniffed her hand, her jeans and her boots before sitting and allowing herself to be petted.

"Such a pretty girl." As she stroked the silky head and buried her fingers in the luxurious ruff, she glanced up at Luke. "I'd forgotten how much I loved being around dogs. We always had them, but Rex was the last one and he died soon after I went to culinary school."

"Unfortunately, we didn't have dogs, or cats, either. Gerbils were about the extent of our pet situation."

"Why was that?"

"The church didn't strictly forbid pets, but the rules and regs were substantial. It would have caused extra hassle so we just didn't."

"So Delilah's your first."

"She's not mine."

"Not yet, but—"

"Someone could still show up."

"If they haven't shown up by now, I doubt they will." She gave Delilah one last scratch before fetching a water bowl from the kitchen. When she set it down, Delilah started drinking. "She looks really happy to be with you. I think she's bonding."

He held her gaze. "If that's the case, what if someone comes for her?"

"Then you'd better hope she loves those people more than she loves you. Otherwise she won't go willingly."

"That could be a mess." His chest heaved. "I had no clue this would get so complicated."

She took pity on him. "It's really not. The chances of someone coming to get her are slim. It's more likely that you and Delilah will live happily ever after."

He smiled. "I like that image."

That smile and his gentle words turned her insides to mush. She wanted to take his face in both hands and kiss that sensuous mouth of his. That wouldn't be very professional but it sure would be more fun than going over her daily receipts, which was what he'd come here to do.

Evidently he remembered that about the same time that she did. "We should get started. Unfortunately, I have a bit of a time crunch."

"Why's that?"

"It has to do with my house." He shrugged out of his sheepskin jacket and walked over to the coat rack. Delilah followed and stood watching as he hooked his coat and his hat on the rack. She stayed beside him as he returned.

He glanced down at her. "Okay, girl. I have work to do. Go lie down."

She trotted over to a spot in the corner and plopped to the floor.

"Clearly Delilah acknowledges you as the alpha dog." Abigail took a seat at the table.

"The *what*?"

"The alpha, the leader of the pack."

"What pack? It's just Delilah and me."

"Even if only two beings are involved, one has to be in charge. Ideally that would be you."

"I suppose." He sat down. "But sometimes she acts like she wants to be in charge. Like over at the ranch she tried to herd me so I'd go stand near Kendra."

Abigail laughed. "Then maybe she has alpha tendencies. That'll keep you on your toes. Make sure you don't allow her to push you around."

"And I thought all I needed to take care of her was food, a leash, a collar and a dog bed."

"That's only the beginning."

"I see that." He pulled out his laptop, flipped it open and glanced at the screen. "We have about half an hour before I need to head home. Trevor and Badger are there working."

"So what's going on with your house?"

"They're sanding the living room floor, but they have to go in less than an hour. I told them I'd be back before they took off."

"Is the floor hardwood, then?"

"Turns out it is. Badger and I pulled up the grungy old living room carpet last night. Then we cut a section out of the carpet in the other rooms. Oak throughout."

"Awesome. Must be exciting to see it transformed."

"It is, but I don't want to shortchange my time with you. If we don't get finished, I'll give them a call."

"I'm sure we can get done. It's just the receipts, right?"

"Not quite. I'd also like a rundown on what you pay everyone. If you can get me a figure for the rent and the latest utility bills, that would be good, too."

"Um...let me check in my office." She hoped she could put her hands on those figures. Although she'd written checks for everything he'd mentioned, she didn't always record them.

She found the checkbook under a pile of papers and flipped through it. The staff was paid every two weeks and the amount fluctuated every month. The rent was a constant, but the utilities fluctuated, too. Some she'd recorded and some she hadn't.

Luke was making notes on his laptop when she came out of the office. She paused. She'd never had a chance to study him when he wasn't aware of it. A handsome guy against a background of Valentine decorations certainly inspired some excellent fantasies—romantic walks in the snow, cozy evenings by the fire, a tender kiss...

Enough. This was a business meeting and he was on a tight schedule. Romance was not on the agenda.

She came around the counter and he looked up from his laptop. His brown gaze warmed, rocketing her back to the moment on the dance floor when he'd held her gently yet firmly in his strong arms.

She broke eye contact. Now wasn't the time. "I found some info for you."

"Good." His tone was crisp. "Let's see what you've got."

She handed over the sheet of paper. Didn't look very official. "I had to estimate on the utilities."

"For now, I just need a general idea. We can get into specifics later."

The word *specifics* made her break out in a cold sweat. She'd operated for the past twelve months on estimates. The estimates had fit into her view of things, which had been soft-focus.

His goal was to sharpen that focus and expose the flaws in her system. The joke was on her that the person who'd make her face the truth about her business was a gorgeous cowboy. She wanted Luke to see her as a competent entrepreneur, not an inept manager of resources.

But it was too late to turn back. Her behavior was under his microscope. Much as she hated that, she needed his evaluation if she expected to keep Pie in the Sky running.

He studied her figures and his eyebrows rose.

She wanted to hide but that wasn't an option. Taking a deep breath, she returned to her chair opposite him. "What's the verdict?"

He gazed at her over his laptop. "Based on your current income and the pay scale you've set up, you can't afford three full-time employees. You need to adjust hours to part-time."

"No." The word popped out. But once it was there, she stood by it. "I can't do that. They all need the money."

His expression gentled. "I understand that you care about them, but if you lose your business, none of them will have a job."

Her throat tightened. "It can't be Ingrid. She's learning to be a baker. It could be a career path for her. Yolanda's putting herself through pharmacy school and besides, she's awesome with customers."

"And the third one?"

"Doug. He's trying to figure things out. This job anchors him while he does that. I can't—"

"He'll still have that, just not as many hours." His voice was kind, but firm. "He can look for another part-time job to make up the difference."

"I don't want to cut anyone's hours. There has to be another way."

"All right. Then create a new revenue stream that justifies those hours. It would be even better if it brings people in during your slow times."

"Like what?"

He massaged the back of his neck. "I'm not sure. Maybe…coffee?"

"I serve coffee."

"But it's just regular coffee, no frills. What if you offered specialty coffee? Made Pie in the Sky a destination for a specialty coffee and a pastry? Offer people espressos, lattes, interesting flavors?"

"I don't know anything about that. And I don't have the equipment."

"You can find some basic equipment that won't cost an arm and a leg. Then train one of your three employees as a barista."

"How can I train them if I know nothing myself?"

"Go online, put your heads together. I'll bet you could figure it out."

"You're giving me a lot of credit."

"Because I know you can do it. You may hate paperwork, but you love pleasing customers. Does anyone else in Eagles Nest serve specialty coffee?"

"Not that I know of." Gradually the concept took hold. He had a point. She'd opened a bakery because the town didn't have one and the customers had flocked in. If she gave them the kind of coffee they couldn't get anywhere else, they'd come to her shop for that, too. "All right. Specialty coffee it is. Sure beats cutting Doug's hours."

He laughed and shook his head. "I hope this guy appreciates your loyalty."

"He might not, but I don't care. He needs the stability of this shop." Which wasn't nearly as stable as Doug thought it was.

"All right then." He closed his laptop. "Getting the coffee thing going will be the goal for this next week. Let me know if you run into any glitches."

"I will. And you need to get back to your house and see how Trevor and Badger are doing." Didn't look as if he planned to ask her out this weekend. Not that she'd expected it. Well, maybe she had. Last Saturday night had been promising.

"I should get going." But he didn't leave the table. "Listen, it's just in the early stages, but would you like to see what we've done so far?"

Being coy wasn't her style. "Great idea. I'll follow you out there."

9

Luke called to alert Badger and Trevor that Abigail was coming out to see the work in progress. Then he spent the rest of the drive explaining to Delilah why he'd made this spur-of-the-moment invitation.

"Hey, she seemed interested in the renovation, so why not let her see what's going on?"

The dog gave him an *I'm not buying it* look.

"Okay so you don't believe me. I don't believe myself, to be honest. The minute I saw her at the bakery today, surrounded by Valentine's decorations and the aroma of fresh pastries, I wanted to kiss her."

Delilah let out a doggie sigh.

"But for the record, I didn't. Didn't even touch her. I'm allowing myself this one little thing—showing her my house. Is that so terrible? Don't answer that."

She didn't. Instead she turned to gaze out the windshield as they neared the house. When he parked in front of it, she quivered with excitement.

Clearly this house had become her touchstone, her reassurance that she had a place where she was wanted and loved. If someone contacted one of the shelters claiming she was their dog, they'd have to prove themselves worthy before he'd turn her over. Delilah would have to be eager to go.

"Bet you're hungry, aren't you, pup?" But that wasn't the whole story.

The first night he'd brought her here, she'd roamed from room to room as he'd stacked logs and kindling in the fireplace. When he'd had the fire crackling, she'd come in and curled up on the rug in front of it. She'd been out like a light.

He'd eaten his dinner sitting on the couch watching her sleep. By the time he'd been ready for bed, she still hadn't moved. Calling himself an idiot, he'd brought blankets and a pillow out to the couch so he could sleep there and tend the fire all night. He'd wanted her to feel safe and warm.

He'd had a crick in his back the next day from sleeping on the couch, so he'd bought her a pet bed and put it at the foot of his bed. She'd taken to it immediately

Difficult though it was to admit, he liked having her around. If someone showed up to claim her, he'd miss her like the devil. Logic said he could adopt another dog, but she wouldn't be Delilah. She wouldn't be the pup with the expressive eyes, the sweet girl he'd coaxed out of a snowstorm and into his truck.

After switching off the engine, he reached over and opened the passenger door so Delilah could hop down and go to her favorite spot to take care of business. He no longer worried about her running off. During the ride on Sunday, she'd never gone more than a few yards away before heading back to him.

Abigail parked her SUV next to his truck. That made quite a nice row of vehicles in front of his house. Like a party. When the house was ready, he'd have one.

Abigail was out of her vehicle before he could get to her door. "Luke, no wonder you bought this place. It's the perfect cabin in the woods."

"I wanted the exact opposite of an apartment in the city."

"You sure got it. I see a chimney. Does that mean you have a working fireplace?"

"I do." When Delilah trotted over and pressed her head against his thigh, he reached down to rub the top of her head and scratch behind her ears.

"Do you use it?"

"Every night." He pictured enjoying a fire with her. Cuddling. Kissing...

"When I get a house, I want a fireplace."

"But a house wouldn't be as convenient as living above the bakery."

"I know." She surveyed his place. "I've considered that. But then I see something like this, with a front porch where you can sit on summer evenings."

"I'm looking forward to that. I need chairs, though." He could invite her out when the weather warmed up. They could listen to the crickets and the owls. Sip a cool drink. But every scenario ended with him taking her into his arms. He ached with the need to do that.

"Rockers. At least that's what I'd get."

"Good idea." The whine of a sander cut into his fantasy. "We'd better go see how those guys are doing."

"Absolutely." She took a deep breath. "Mm. I can smell the sawdust from out here."

"Because all the caulking needs to be replaced. The house leaks like a sieve." He motioned to the porch steps. "After you. The door's unlocked."

"Do they know I'm coming?"

"Yes, ma'am. Called them on the way here." He patted his thigh. "Let's go, Delilah." He followed Abigail into the house.

Earlier he'd helped Trevor and Badger cram all the living room furniture into the dining room. Then he'd turned on the overhead so they could see what they were doing. The setting was a little stark, but the floor looked great. Finished, in fact. He hadn't expected that.

Trevor, wearing goggles and a face mask, switched off the sander and pulled down the mask. "Hi, you two. Welcome to the floor that's smooth as a baby's butt."

"Or will be once I finish vacuumin' up the sawdust," Badger said. "Evenin', Miss Abigail."

"Hey, Badger."

Luke glanced at her. "I take it you've met this guy."

"Sure have. He's the reason I added pecan pie to the menu."

"And you make it just like my granny did," Badger said. "Now if y'all will stay right there for a minute, I'll get rid of the sawdust."

"Sure." Luke looked down at Delilah. "Sit."

She obeyed, but her body quivered with eagerness. She took her role as official greeter seriously.

Badger turned on the shop vac and took care of the sawdust Trevor had left with his last pass. Then he shut it down. "That should do 'er." He swept an arm around the empty room. "Behold."

"Then you're finished with the sanding?"

Trevor surveyed the bare floor. "With this room. Goes fast with power tools."

"I sanded part of it." Badger looked proud of himself. "That section over there by the fireplace. That's my work."

"It looks amazing. I just didn't expect you to be done already. I was planning to help."

Delilah's soft whine reminded him she was sitting not-so-patiently by his side. "Okay, girl. You can get up."

She stood, surveyed the situation and went to Trevor.

"Guess she loves you best," Badger said.

"'Course she does." He grinned. "All the ladies do, right, Delilah?" He took off his goggles and crouched down to pet her. Then he glanced up at Luke. "Don't worry about not pitching in on this section. There's still plenty to do."

"It's beautiful. Once you varnish it, that wood will glow like honey." Abigail unzipped her parka.

"Let me take your coat." Luke shrugged out of his jacket. The house needed work but the furnace was new and kept the place toasty warm.

"That's okay. I wasn't planning to stay."

"Don't leave on our account." Trevor stood. "We're done for the day." When he walked into the dining room, Delilah transferred her attention to Badger.

"So I'm second best." Badger leaned down to scratch behind her ears. "Just don't forget that I'm the one who gave you that awesome name."

"It's a good name." Trevor returned with his coat and hat. "Want us to help you put some of the furniture back?"

Luke shook his head. "Thanks, but let's just leave it. Are you still available to put a coat of varnish on it tomorrow?"

"Absolutely." Trevor glanced at Abigail. "Get Luke to show you around before you leave. It's a sweet little house. A little TLC and it'll be—" He paused and looked down. Delilah had walked over and started nudging him toward the door. "Hey, pup, I'm going, I'm going. I can take a hint."

Badger cracked up. "Hey, Trev, she's givin' you the bum's rush. Guess she doesn't love you best after all."

"That's not it," Luke said. "She's herding him over to Abigail and me. She wants us in a cluster. Stay there, Badger. She'll come for you next."

"This I gotta see."

Delilah gave Trevor one more nudge before turning toward Badger.

"Get ready," Luke said. "Here she comes."

"Well, I'll be damned." Badger allowed himself to be maneuvered toward the door. "I've never seen the like."

"I have," Trevor said. "But I'd forgotten it. One of my buddies in high school had a border collie mix who used to do that. A bunch of us would go to his house and spread out in the yard so he'd launch into his routine." He buttoned his coat. "I'm outta here. Olivia and I are having date night and she's already started dinner. Nice seeing you Abigail."

"Same here, Trevor. The floor looks awesome."

"Yeah, it does, Trev," Luke added. "Thank you so much."

"You're welcome. See you in the morning."

After Trevor left, Badger pulled out his phone and checked the time. "I should be takin' off, too. I have a hot phone date with Hayley in about thirty minutes and I doubt you want to listen in while I'm sweet-talkin' your sister."

Luke rolled his eyes. "You've got that right."

"Otherwise I'd stay and partake of the chili your mama dropped off while you were gone. She makes amazin' chili."

"My mom was here?"

"She was. Left the chili as a thank you for givin' her the idea of buyin' a barn. She found one. 'Scuse me while I go fetch my coat and hat."

"She found a venue?" Luke called after him. "That's great!" Luke blessed his good timing or his mother's bad timing. Either way, she hadn't arrived to find Abigail here. That was for the best.

Abigail looked confused. "Why would you suggest that your mom needs a barn?"

"She's been wanting to expand her business. I thought buying an old barn and fixing it up as a wedding venue would be a good way to go. Anyone who rents it will probably use her services. She has to get financing, but that shouldn't be too hard."

Badger came back out, buttoning his coat on the way. "I'm investin' in it."

"Are you, now? Luke smiled. "Smart move."

"I know what you're thinkin', that I'm tryin' to butter her up."

"Yep."

"Don't need to. Your momma already dotes on me. And she's goin' to clean up with this barn concept. It'll be more popular than a beehive in a bear wallow."

Abigail laughed. "I just love hearing you talk, Badger."

"Thank you kindly. As it happens, I love talkin'. Now if you two will excuse me, I'll head on home to make that phone call to my darlin'."

"Tell her hi for me," Luke said.

"I'll do that, Luke. Miss Abigail." He tipped his hat in her direction and headed out the door.

"Badger's fun." Abigail pulled up the tab of her zipper. "I should be going, too."

She was leaving. Letting her go was safer. To hell with safe. "Since my mom brought over chili, would you like to stay and have some with me?"

Her smile bloomed. "That sounds wonderful."

<u>10</u>

While Delilah ate her dog food and the chili warmed on the stove, Abigail enjoyed a tour of the house. With only two bedrooms and one bathroom, plus the dining room and kitchen, the tour didn't take long. About halfway through, Delilah came looking for them and stayed by Luke's side until they returned to the kitchen.

"See?" Abigail gestured to the pup. "Bonded."

"Or maybe she wants more food."

"She might, but I think it's you she's after." Abigail understood. Hanging out with Luke and watching him be domestic was a treat. "Your house is extremely cozy."

"Thanks. It has a ways to go, yet, but I like it." He lifted the lid on the chili. "Coming along."

"Smells terrific."

"It's my favorite. My mom must be super happy about that barn to have made this for me." Luke glanced down at Delilah when she nudged his thigh. "You've had your dinner, girl. Go lie down."

The dog padded over to a corner of the kitchen. Then she flopped down with her head on her paws and her gaze fixed on Luke.

Abigail chuckled at the worshipful expression in the dog's eyes. "She's in love."

"She's hoping for a dog biscuit. But she's getting plenty of treats these days."

"She can't help being adorable." She turned back to him. "So are weddings in barns popular?"

"That's what my research showed. I can't help noticing wedding stuff since I grew up with a mom who lives and breathes them."

"I've never known a wedding planner. How was that?"

"Hayley and I got slightly phobic. When we were little we were sometimes recruited to be the flower girl and the ring bearer." Tapping the spoon on the pot, he laid it in a spoon rest. "She hates anything with lace on it and I'd rather not wear a tux if I can avoid it. But Mom's business thrived in Colorado Springs."

"I can also see why it would slow down in a town this size, though."

"She figured it wouldn't be anything like what she had and she was right. Hiring someone to plan a lavish wedding is an urban thing." He opened a cupboard and took out a bottle of red wine. "How about this to go with the chili?"

"Perfect."

He took an opener from a drawer and pulled out the cork. "Mom says many folks in Eagles Nest plan their own wedding, bake their own cake and pick wildflowers for the bouquets."

"I realized that when I got here. It's the reason I haven't pushed elaborate wedding cakes. They take a lot of work and cost more than a regular cake. I just do one if somebody asks."

"But the barn venue will attract out-of-towners. That could be an opportunity for you." He searched the cupboards and finally came up with a couple of wine glasses.

"I suppose it could." She had trouble keeping her attention on the conversation. Sharing space with Luke in this intimate setting had put her senses on high alert.

A week ago she'd postponed a kiss until she was more rested. She'd been up since three this time, too. But she'd never been more awake, more aware of every move he made.

As he rinsed and dried the wine glasses, she focused on his strong, capable hands. She imagined him stroking her cheek, cupping her chin, tilting her face up to his...

"A successful venue could end up hosting four or five weddings per weekend and several more during the week if the location catches on. Mom's will do great."

She caught enough of what he'd said to respond semi-intelligently. "Because you'll see to it?"

He flashed her a smile. "I'll do my best."

He took her breath away. She was in danger of standing there gaping at him because he was just that gorgeous. "You...um...sound very confident."

"I know my job." Picking up the wine bottle, he filled the glasses.

"Have you been researching bakeries, too?"

"I have." He recorked the wine. "But I had a head start after working for a restaurant chain. Some of the principles are the same."

"What would I have done if you hadn't decided to move here?"

His gaze met hers. "I don't like to think about it."

"Me, either." *Breathe, girl.*

He handed her a glass. "Here's to a healthy profit margin."

She almost laughed. Profit margins were the last thing on her mind. "I'll drink to that." She touched her glass to his and took a sip. "Mm. Nice."

"I didn't bring much from Portland, but I hauled down a couple of cases of Oregon wine." He glanced at the chili bubbling in the pot. "It's ready."

"Good." Eating would give her something to do besides stare at him. Evidently he hadn't noticed her besotted state.

"I didn't think this through, though. The dining room is crowded with furniture and...you know what? How about spreading a blanket on the living room floor? I could make a fire."

Be still my beating heart. "That sounds fabulous. What can I do?"

He took two bowls from the cupboard. "Dish the chili, please." He grabbed a tray from a bottom shelf. "You can bring it in on this. I'll take the wine and rustle us up a fire." He left the kitchen.

Delilah got to her feet and followed him. But soon she trotted back into the kitchen and began nudging Abigail while she was dishing the chili. "Cut it out, Delilah. I'll make a mess." With adrenaline coursing through her system, she was already less coordinated. Delilah's pestering didn't help.

The nudging continued.

"Luke," she called out. "Your dog's trying to herd me into the living room. I'm liable to dump chili everywhere."

"Delilah, come!"

The dog started out of the kitchen, but kept glancing back in a clear request for her to follow.

"In a minute, girl. When I've finished dishing the chili."

With a little doggie sigh, Delilah left the kitchen.

A few seconds later, Luke began to laugh. "Now she's trying to get me to go back in there with you."

"Hang on. I'm almost done." She set the bowls on the tray along with a couple of spoons she'd found and some paper napkins. Then she carried everything into the living room.

Her breath caught and she gripped the tray to keep from dropping it. Romantic fantasies did come true, after all. Luke had turned off the overhead so the room was lit only by the glow of flames dancing in the fireplace and the ambient light from the kitchen. A colorful quilt lay on the smooth floor.

He placed a folding mesh screen in front of the fire and turned to her with another one of those bone-melting smiles. The fantasy was complete.

He walked toward her. "Let me take that."

"Okay." She sounded breathless. Couldn't help it.

After setting the tray in the middle of the quilt, he glanced at Delilah and pointed to a corner of it. "Lie down, girl."

She walked to where he'd pointed and flopped down with a contented sigh.

He chuckled. "Are you happy, pup, now that Abigail and I are together?"

The dog gazed up at him and her tail thumped the floor.

Delilah wasn't the only happy one. Abigail resisted the urge to pinch herself as she surveyed the cozy setting. "This is lovely. Thank you for inviting me to stay."

"I'm glad you said yes." He gestured toward the quilt. "Have a seat."

"You'd better take the spot closest to Delilah." She sat on the far side of the tray. "That fire smells so good."

"It's cedar."

"And the rock fireplace is beautiful."

"It's also well-built. Whoever did it knew their stonework." He took the opposite side of the tray and handed over her wine glass. "That's a part of the house that's fine the way it is. I had to clean out a bird's nest, but otherwise it's in great shape."

"Are you keeping the knotty pine paneling?" She picked up her bowl of chili.

"Definitely. I like the retro feel of it."

"So do I. It gives everything a warm glow." She tasted her chili. "Wow, I can see why this is your favorite. It's delicious."

"Sure is. Especially when you're sitting in front of a fire. Seems twice as good."

"I wouldn't know since I've never had your mom's chili before, but this is yummy." Good food, good wine, a crackling fire and Luke sitting within arm's reach. She was on sensory overload.

After eating a few more bites, she put down the bowl and picked up her wine glass. "This is going to be an awesome house."

"I think so, too. I've dreamed about a place like this ever since I was a kid. We went on a family vacation one year and rented a cabin near some state park or other. This reminds me of it."

"I can see why. My family rented a vacation cabin that was something like this, too. Only it was near a lake."

"There's no lake close by, but Wild Creek isn't far. It's mostly frozen, now, but in the summer, I'll bet I'll be able to hear it if I sit on the porch."

"In a rocker."

He smiled at her. "Exactly."

"I'm happy for you, Luke. It must feel terrific to have found the place of your dreams." She spooned up the last of her chili and put the bowl on the tray.

"It does."

"Think of all the fires you'll enjoy." She wrapped her arms around her knees and stared into the flames. "Watching how they burn is mesmerizing."

"Uh-huh."

Something in his voice made her glance at him.

He wasn't watching the fire. He was looking at her. "More wine?"

"No, thank you." Her heart began to pound.

"Then let's move this." Picking up the tray, he lifted it over his knees and set it down on his other side. "It's in the way."

"Of what?" As if she didn't know. As if she didn't recognize the heat that simmered in his eyes.

He turned to face her. "Scoot around, okay?"

She moved so her bent knees touched his.

"That's better." He took both her hands in his. "Ever since Badger left, I've wanted to kiss you." He stroked the backs of her hands with his thumbs.

She swallowed. "Ever since Badger left, I've been hoping you would."

Releasing her hands, he cupped her face and gazed into her eyes. "Good to know." Urging her closer with easy pressure, he placed a soft kiss on her forehead.

She closed her eyes, heart thrumming, as his butterfly kisses brushed her eyelids, then her cheeks. He lingered there, igniting little bursts of pleasure with each caress.

As he gently kissed the corners of her mouth, she quivered in anticipation. *Soon.* Then his warm lips settled over hers.

And the world as she knew it changed forever.

11

Luke touched down lightly, cherishing the sensation of her lips, velvet and pliant. *Abigail.* Her breath hitched and her cheeks warmed beneath his fingers. Slowly he increased the pressure. A shiver of recognition ran through him, as if he'd found the key to a treasure he'd secretly longed for yet never expected to find.

Gently he parted her lips with the tip of his tongue. He tasted a sweetness, a promise of delights he'd only glimpsed in dreams, a richness to be savored, celebrated.

She moaned softly as he shifted the angle, taking his time, drawing out the pleasure. Slowly. Gently. The perfection, the absolute rightness stunned him. He paused, heart racing, and drew back to gaze at her flushed face, her moist lips.

Her lashes lay still, then fluttered upward to reveal eyes filled with wonder. Her gaze was so open, so vulnerable.

He tried to speak. Couldn't. Cleared his throat. "That was..." He shook his head. "I didn't expect...

"I know." She sounded breathless.

His heart continued to pound. Every word, every gesture, was critical, as if he'd been given a package marked *Handle with Care.* "I don't want to mess this up."

"Me, either."

Slowly he released her. "Then maybe we should—"

"Take a break?"

He nodded. "But I want to see you again. Soon."

"Absolutely." She started to get up.

He stood and helped her to her feet. "How's Sunday?" His brain might resemble a jar of Mexican jumping beans but he was determined to have a plan before she left.

"I'll need to do some baking in the afternoon, but my morning's free."

"Do you ride?"

"If I have a gentle horse. I haven't been on one for a while, though, so I might be rusty."

"We won't push it, and Wild Creek Ranch is chockablock with gentle horses. Kendra and I were going out Sunday morning. Will you come with us?"

"I'd love to."

"Great. We were planning to leave about ten if that works for you. But maybe you like to sleep in on your day off."

She smiled. "Oh, I sleep in. I don't get up until five on Sundays."

"That late, huh? Lazybones."

"In any case, I can be at the ranch by ten."

"Then it's a plan." He fetched her parka from the coat closet near the door and held it while she slipped her arms into the sleeves.

Her warmth called to him. He longed to pull her close, but caution lights flashed in his brain. If he rushed this, he could ruin it.

Delilah roused herself and trotted over to the door, tail wagging.

Abigail crouched down and stroked the dog's thick fur. "See you later, girl." She glanced up at him. "Will you bring her on Sunday?"

"Definitely. She loves it."

"I'm sure I will, too." She stood, zipped her parka and put up the hood. "See you both Sunday morning. Thank you for dinner and—"

"The tour?" He smiled.

"Right." Her attention lingered on his mouth and her breathing quickened. "And...everything. 'Bye, Luke."

"'Bye, Abigail."

But as she reached for the knob, Delilah blocked the door. "Omigod, that's so sweet! She doesn't want me to go."

The dog must be channeling him. "Delilah, come."

She surveyed them both before walking slowly to his side.

"See you soon," Abigail murmured as she slipped through the opening and closed the door behind her.

The second she was gone, he missed her like the devil.

Delilah whined and gave him a sad-eyed look that said he'd screwed up. Now she had to make do with only one human instead of two.

"Yeah, well, you slept through the significant part of the evening, pup, so I can't expect you to understand." Outside, an engine started, revved up. Then the rumble gradually faded as Abigail drove away.

He took a deep breath. "And I have a call to make." Carrying the tray of bowls and glasses into the kitchen, he located his phone and called Kendra.

She answered right away. "Hey, Luke! What's up?"

"Not much. I didn't know if I'd catch you on a Friday night."

"You can catch me most nights unless the Whine and Cheese Club has called a meeting. What's your excuse? You should be kicking up your heels at the GG right now."

"Not tonight. Hey, I have a request regarding our ride Sunday morning."

"Shoot."

"Is it okay if Abigail goes along?"

"Of course. How experienced is she?"

"She's ridden, but not recently. She'd need someone gentle, but all yours are well-trained. Any would work."

"True, but Strawberry's her best bet. I'll make sure he's available for Sunday morning. Same time?"

"Same time." He hesitated. "How much do you know about her background?"

"Not much. Why?"

"Well, because both of her parents are gone and I—"

"Gone? You mean they died?"

"Yes, about five years ago. And she's an only child. She used her inheritance to open the bakery."

"I had no idea her parents weren't alive! She's so young to be on her own. What about grandparents, aunts, uncles?"

"She didn't mention any. Not everyone has extended family who can step in."

Kendra took a deep breath. "So true. I didn't."

"I know."

"I didn't realize we had that in common. I'm glad you told me."

"She seems resilient, though. Like you."

"You have to be. Either that or give in to victim mentality. I don't see her that way, either. Listen, why don't you guys stay for lunch? It'll give me a chance to get to know her better."

"Are you sure you have time?"

"I'll make time, assuming she's available."

"Then I'll ask and let you know. Lunch would be nice."

"Everything going okay?"

He took a breath. "I think so."

"I'm glad you're bringing her on the ride. You have good instincts, Luke. Just follow them and you'll be fine."

"Thanks for the vote of confidence. See you Sunday."

***

So much had happened since arriving at Luke's house that Abigail was surprised it was only seven-thirty when she got home. Normally she went to bed by eight, but she was too wired tonight.

After hanging up her coat, she texted Roxanne and discovered she was giving Ingrid a foot massage. Roxanne told her to come on down.

She walked over to Roxanne's, tapped on her door and went in. None of them locked up because the door at the foot of the stairs was all that counted. It had a steel core and a deadbolt. That was enough security for Eagles Nest.

Roxanne had pulled her mass of dark hair into a ponytail. She'd brought a kitchen chair in and positioned herself in front of Ingrid, who sat on the couch, her foot in Roxanne's lap. She glanced over at Abigail. "Hey, girlfriend. Where've you been?"

"How do you know I was gone?" She pulled over a bean bag chair and settled into it.

"We checked." Ingrid put down her mug on the side table. "Want some herbal tea? I bought some today and it's very soothing."

"No, thanks."

"Then get Roxanne to massage your feet. She's studied reflexology and she's good at it."

"I'll bet she is, but I'm heading off to bed soon."

Ingrid yawned. "Me, too. After this I'll sleep like a baby. Did you go out to dinner?"

"Luke wanted to show me his house. We ate there."

"Aha!" Roxanne switched to Ingrid's other foot. "That sounds like it could have turned into something."

Only the most incredible first kiss she'd ever encountered. Her mouth still tingled. He'd taken his time, as if he'd been granted a great privilege, as if he cherished every moment his lips were touching hers, as if nothing was more important than pleasing—

"Abigail?"

"What?" She blinked.

Ingrid was peering at her. "You left us for a while, there, girlfriend. *Did* something happen?"

"He kissed me."

Roxanne rolled her eyes and sighed. "And it was awful. Sorry. Nobody that cute should be a bad kisser."

"I don't think he *is* bad, Rox. She was all dreamy and smiling when she took that little mental vacay."

"Then I'm totally confused." Roxanne studied her. "You were at his house and evidently he delivered on the first kiss. And that's it? End of story?"

"We're not rushing things." It was too special to rush. She sighed. "I kind of wish he didn't have to dig into my finances, though. There's nothing romantic about that."

"*Does* he have to dig into them?" Roxanne paused to pour a fragrant oil into the palm of her hand. "Couldn't he just give you some marketing advice and let it go at that?"

"No."

"Why not?"

Abigail gazed at her friends. "It's time I told you the whole story." She stood. "But first I'll fix some of that soothing tea." This wouldn't be easy, but Ingrid deserved to know. She was smart. She might already suspect.

Minutes later, armed with her drink, she sat in the bean bag chair and confessed the state of her finances and the sorry condition of her records.

"Oh, dear." Ingrid looked stricken. "There were times I wondered how you were keeping track, but I was hoping...anyway, it doesn't matter. Take back that raise you gave me when I started baking. I'll be fine with what you were paying me before."

Abigail shook her head. "I'm not reducing what I pay you. You earn every penny and then some. We'll keep your paycheck as is."

"But—"

"You're not going to suffer because of my failings. I'll fix this because it's my fault for not being better organized."

Roxanne paused the massage long enough to glance over at Abigail. "Does Luke know your records aren't in order?"

"I'm sure he suspects, but we haven't come to that point in the process. He's not going to like what he finds." A knot of anxiety in her stomach tightened.

"Do you think he'll judge you?"

"Maybe."

Ingrid picked up her mug of tea. "Just so you know, I don't. You're an awesome baker and you've never owned a business before. I understand how this could happen."

"That's very generous of you. But like I said, I'm not going to let this sink us. Luke won't, either. He came up with another idea to boost revenue. I'm not sure it will work, but I—"

Ingrid sat forward. "What is it?"

"Specialty coffee."

Her eyes widened. "Yeah? Would you do that?"

"Maybe. But I'll have to buy some equipment and one of us will need to learn how to be a barista. And fast. That could get tricky."

Ingrid grinned. "Got that covered."

"What do you mean?"

"I already know how."

"You never told me that!"

"No reason to. If you'd had a typical job application for me to fill out, you'd already know it."

Abigail waved a hand. "Hate those things. Hate filling them out and hate reading them. I prefer just chatting with someone."

"Me, too, but it meant you didn't find out about my past job experience."

"And you were a barista?"

"Yes, ma'am. And I'm damn good at it, too."

"Hallelujah."

Roxanne reached for a pair of warm socks and put them on Ingrid's feet. "You're done."

"Thanks, Rox."

"You're most welcome. But now you need to put on your barista hat and help find a coffee machine." She got up and crossed to her computer.

"I can do that."

Abigail climbed out of the bean bag chair. "Just to get an idea, right? Tomorrow after I close up I can drive to Bozeman and buy something."

"Not efficient." Roxanne woke up her computer and turned back to Abigail. "You'll use time better spent organizing your space to accommodate this new offering."

"Yes, but I have to wait for it to get here."

"Not long these days. I'm the queen of online shopping and we have our barista here to advise us. Together we'll find you a great deal on the best machine with free shipping and fast delivery. See if we don't."

Abigail laughed. "Clearly I haven't been making use of the resources at my disposal. That sounds awesome."

"It will be." Ingrid headed over to the computer desk. "Go get your credit card while we start looking."

"Yes, ma'am." By the time she returned, they'd found the perfect deal at the perfect price.

"It'll be here Tuesday!" Ingrid looked like a kid on Christmas morning. "I can't wait to get my hands on it. I love making all that fun stuff."

"But when will you have time?" Abigail saw pitfalls everywhere. "You're an apprentice baker."

"So I'll be super busy at first."

"You deserve another raise."

"And I'll ask for one once everything settles down. In the meantime, I'll train all of you on the machine so everyone can use it. Don't worry. We'll figure a way to cover our bases."

"It's worth doing." Roxanne exited the site. "That's about the only thing I've missed living here. Eagles Nest is ready for this." She brought up a new screen. "Let's design your coffee menu."

The knot in Abigail's stomach began to loosen. "You know what? This is going to work."

12

Sunday morning. Hot damn. Luke had invited Abigail to stay for lunch and she'd accepted. Kendra was thrilled. It was shaping up to be an awesome day.

He loaded Delilah into the truck and climbed behind the wheel. "We're off, girl." As he shoved the key in the ignition, his phone rang. He picked it up and glanced at the screen. *Heart of the Valley Animal Shelter.*

They'd never called him. He'd checked in with all the organizations in the area a bunch of times, but this was the first instance anyone had contacted him. He glanced at Delilah, who was sitting upright, eagerly awaiting their next adventure. His gut tightened as he answered the call.

"Mr. Bennett?"

"Yes."

The woman identified herself. "Do you still have the border collie mix?"

"Yes." His stomach twisted.

"You asked us to notify you of anything that might pertain to the dog and we have something, but it's inconclusive."

"What is it?"

Delilah gazed at him, worry in her golden eyes. He reached over and stroked her silky head.

"We came across a flyer that appears to describe the animal you have, but there's no picture. It's also been out in the weather and the last three digits of the phone number are unreadable."

Someone had tried to find her. He'd always believed that would happen. She was too amazing to have been discarded like an unwanted toy. Yet whoever it was hadn't persisted. Why?

"I checked the area code and whoever posted the flyer has a San Diego number."

"San Diego?" He had a tough time imagining her as a California dog. She enjoyed the snow too much.

"Let me read you the description."

"All right." The description fit her to a T. The timeframe matched, too. "That's..." He stopped to take a breath. "That's gotta be her."

"But we don't have the whole number."

"I understand that. But they would have posted more than one flyer." A dull ache worked its way from the base of his skull to his temples.

"Logically, yes."

"Then all we need is for someone to find a flyer with a complete number."

"That's true, although Montana weather being what it is, I doubt that will happen. Is there any problem with you keeping her for the time being?"

"There's no problem with me keeping her, period. She's a great dog."

The line went silent for a moment. "I really doubt any more flyers will show up." She sounded kind.

"But let me know if they do."

"I will." The woman wished him well and disconnected.

He stared at the phone. Why would someone go to the trouble of posting flyers and not follow up with calls to the various animal shelters? The numbers were all on the Internet. But they might not be online. Flyers without a picture indicated they weren't tech savvy.

He glanced at Delilah. "I can't figure this out, pup."

She gave him her sad-eyed look.

"Basically we're in limbo, and that sucks." He gave her one final scratch behind her ears. "But we have to get moving or we'll be late."

On the drive to the ranch he took several deep breaths to ease the tightness in his chest but his headache refused to go away.

Although he'd been checking with the shelters on a regular basis, lately he'd done it out of habit. Each call that yielded nothing had helped convince him that everyone was right. He'd get to keep Delilah.

But now.... *San Diego.* So far away. Or maybe they'd moved and that was their cell number. If her people lived around here and they came to claim her, he might get visiting privileges.

On the other hand, if they were in the process of moving, she could end up anywhere. He might never see her again. The iron band around his chest was back.

When he pulled up to the barn, Kendra had all three horses at the hitching post and was grooming a tall bay named Jake. She'd probably chosen Jake for herself.

He let Delilah out before he climbed down. The pup trotted over to Kendra, tail wagging and a mile-wide doggie smile on her face.

Kendra laid aside her brush. "If it isn't my new best friend!"

Delilah whined and wiggled as Kendra scrubbed her gloved hands over the dog's back and told her she was beautiful.

His bad news stuck in his throat. Maybe he wouldn't say anything. No point in saddling Kendra with this. "She sure loves coming over here. When we turned onto the ranch road, she couldn't sit still."

"Is that right, Delilah?" Kendra crouched down and ruffled the dog's floppy ears. "Are you excited to come see your Aunt Kendra? 'Cause I'm excited to see you, too!" She reached in her pocket.

"Oh, boy." Luke managed a weak chuckle as Kendra pulled out a dog biscuit. "I see how it is. She won't want to go home, now."

"Sure she will." Kendra gave Delilah the treat and smiled as she stood to face him. "She likes me fine but she's devoted to you. Which reminds me. Have you heard from anybody?"

"Uh..."

Her forehead wrinkled. "Luke, what's wrong?"

"Heart of the Valley called this morning."

"And?"

He told her about the flyer.

She took a deep breath. "Okay, that's upsetting, but whoever put out the flyer can't be very invested in locating her, can they? You don't just put out a flyer, in bad weather, no less, and then forget about it. You call around."

"But they could be in the process of relocating. They might—"

"I don't care if they've relocated to Timbuktu! You get on the Internet, you find all the shelters in the area where you lost the dog and you call. This is a member of the family we're talking about!"

A weight lifted from his shoulders. "You're right. You're so right."

"Of course I am."

"I want to believe her people love her and can't wait to get her back. But they sure aren't acting like they give a damn. Even if they don't have Internet access, they can find somebody who does."

"Exactly!" She cupped Delilah's jaw and gazed into her eyes. "You're amazing. And we love you to pieces."

"Yeah." Luke cleared his throat. "And if another flyer shows up with a readable number, I'm grilling those people. She's not going anywhere unless they have a damn good reason why they haven't followed up on this."

She kissed Delilah on the top of her head and straightened. "Excellent." She glanced toward the road as a vehicle approached. "I'll bet that's Abigail."

"It is. I'll go meet her."

"Ask her to park up by the house, since you'll be staying for lunch."

"Yes, ma'am." He walked toward Abigail's SUV as she drove in and Delilah came along. Evidently the possibility of another dog biscuit wasn't enough to make her stay with Kendra. He kind of liked knowing that.

After waving to get Abigail's attention, he pointed toward the area near the house where Kendra's truck was parked. He hadn't been thinking about lunch or he would have left his there, too.

Abigail pulled her white SUV in, shut off the motor and got out. Delilah charged over to meet her with even more enthusiasm than she'd shown with Kendra. Interesting.

Crouching, she loved on the dog for a while before glancing up at him. "I brought gloves but I don't have a hat, just my hood. The boots aren't riding boots but they have a heel."

"You'll be fine. This'll be a mellow outing, as requested." Seeing her again just naturally put a big old smile on his face. "Kendra thought you'd want to park here since you'll be staying for lunch."

"Good idea." She zipped her parka as she stood and walked toward him. Her rosy cheeks could be due to the cold breeze, but if her pulse was acting up like his, then it was excitement creating that flush, not chilly weather.

The last time they'd been together...no, better not focus on that right now. "How've you been?"

"Great! You won't believe this, but Ingrid's a trained barista."

"No kidding! That's terrific."

"You're telling me. The coffee machine will arrive Tuesday. Ingrid wants a day to familiarize herself, but we plan to be brewing specialty coffee first thing Thursday morning."

"I'm impressed."

"Me, too. Friday night I finally broke down and explained my financial situation to both Ingrid and Roxanne and they've been so—"

"Ingrid didn't know?"

"Since I didn't want to face it, I certainly wasn't going to tell her. I think she suspected something, though, especially when I hired you."

"Thinking back on it, I'm a little surprised you did."

"Self-preservation finally kicked in. And I knew immediately you were kind. You walked into the GG with a dog you'd just rescued."

"She's a gift that keeps on giving." Might as well not mention the flyer. It didn't loom as large now that he'd talked with Kendra. "Anyway, I'm impressed that you're moving so quickly on the coffee."

"Turns out it was easier than I thought." She smiled at him. "I'm glad you suggested this, Luke. I was nervous when I was driving here. I thought maybe we'd be awkward with each other after Friday night. But we're not, are we?"

"No, ma'am." But he couldn't wait for the right moment to kiss her again.

* * *

Abigail had told the truth. Her nervousness about seeing Luke today had disappeared to be replaced by a deep longing to be held in those strong arms.

He'd always been a good-looking cowboy in his Stetson. But when he'd mounted Spot On, his handsome Appaloosa, he'd transformed into a dream come true. He owned every bit of sexiness attached to the cowboy fantasy. Abigail could watch him forever.

That turned out to be impossible. Kendra led the trail ride and Abigail was assigned the middle spot. It made sense because she was the least experienced rider. But she had to dream up reasons to say something to Luke just to give her an excuse to scoot around and get a look at him.

And to enjoy Delilah's antics, too. She was having the time of her life. Mostly she stuck close to Luke and Spot On. But every so often she'd see something of interest off the trail and bound through the drifts to investigate.

She'd come back with snow sticking to her muzzle like a fake beard, which always made Luke grin.

Abigail was so entranced by Luke, his dog and his horse, that twice she'd lost a stirrup while twisting in the saddle, but she'd covered that well. Maybe. When she'd nearly tumbled off, though, she'd given up trying to glance back at him. Falling from a horse that was only walking down the trail would be damned embarrassing.

Her gelding, a roan aptly named Strawberry, was a sweetheart. He ambled along at a pace that would have been relaxing if she hadn't been focused on the manly cowboy riding behind her. The one who could kiss like nobody's business.

Because Kendra could turn in the saddle without losing a stirrup or her balance, she did that periodically to check on her guests. Abigail appreciated it. Kendra had a reputation for providing the safest trail rides in the area and her skills were on display this morning.

Her tone was calm and cheerful as she asked about prior experience with horses, how the saddle felt and whether she liked the horse she was on.

"Strawberry's perfect for me," Abigail said. "How long have you had him?"

"About eight years."

"How long have you been offering trail rides?"

"Let me think. I started when Jo Fielding and I became friends. She offered to watch my boys on the weekends so I could add trail rides to the mix. Prior to that I was only boarding. I guess we're talking more than twenty-five years."

"And business has been steady?"

Kendra chuckled. "People in business for themselves don't generally use the word *steady*. They accept the peaks and valleys and work through them."

That was an eye-opener. "Pie in the Sky hasn't had any valleys, yet." Just the cliff that loomed ahead, the one she was determined not to go over.

"Then you're lucky. Maybe you won't experience fluctuations. Bakeries could be different. With my business, it depends on so many variables—airline fares, weather, the economy, the cost of feed, competition from other stables, the general mood of the country. It all factors in."

"I chose Eagles Nest because I wouldn't have competition. But I see what you mean. This has been a good year, but I'm new in town. Still a novelty."

"That never hurts." Kendra reined in the tall bay she was riding, turned around and called out to Luke. "Let's head back!"

"Got it!"

"Want to lead?"

"Sure, why not?" He glanced up at the sky. "Think it's gonna snow?"

"Any minute, now. But we'll be fine. It's fun to ride when it's snowing." Kendra glanced at her. "Have you ever done it?"

"Never. I've only ridden in the summer."

"Then you're in for a treat. I don't recommend going out in a blizzard, but that's not what the weather channel predicted. Just follow Luke. He'll lead us back home."

He'd pulled up his horse and was waiting for them. "You doing okay, Abigail?"

"I'm doing fabulously, Luke."

He smiled. "Glad to hear it. I thought you might like this."

"I do. Very much." Oh, yeah, she liked it all right, especially when he gave her a smile that lit her up inside.

Flakes drifted down, placing cool kisses on her cheeks and gathering in Strawberry's mane. The horses' breath fogged the air as Luke clucked to the gelding and wheeled him around. She nudged Strawberry forward.

Enclosed in a snow-globe world, she kept her gaze on the broad-shouldered cowboy riding ahead of her on the black and white Appaloosa. He sat easy in the saddle, one gloved hand on the reins and the other resting on his thigh. Snow dusted his sheepskin jacket, his black Stetson and the spotted rump of his horse.

She'd happily follow this cowboy... anywhere.

13

Luke had been a fan of riding through snow ever since he could remember. Nothing beat being out in it, especially if it wasn't a brutal storm. Coming inside to build a fire and heat up a meal was the perfect finish to a chilly ride.

Abigail's obvious enjoyment sharpened his pleasure. Exactly what he'd been going for—a chance to share an experience that had nothing to do with her business or his. Kendra had told him to follow his instincts, and in this case, he'd made a good call.

Delilah had loved being out there, too. She was one wet dog when Luke carried her into the laundry room to dry her off with the towels Kendra gave him. By the time he'd made the pup suitable for lying on Kendra's hardwood floor, Kendra and Abigail had built a fire, warmed the stew and brewed coffee.

They brought their meal into the living room so they could gather around the fire. Delilah chose a place near the hearth, Kendra settled into an easy chair and Luke joined Abigail on the couch.

"Perfect timing." Kendra glanced out the window. "It's coming down harder, now."

"I feel like a pioneer woman," Abigail said. "Here we sit by the fire sheltered by the walls of a log cabin. Or a log ranch house, I guess you'd have to say."

"I've always loved that about this place." Kendra glanced around. "I've lived here for so long that sometimes I forget how special it is. Thanks for reminding me. It's probably the coziest in weather like this."

"I'm glad you heat the barns." Abigail cradled her coffee mug in both hands. "It's nice to know the horses are all snug and warm, too."

"They'd be fine if we didn't heat it, though. We're spoiling them a little, but I'm a softie when it comes to our animals."

"What about the chickens?" Luke had seen the elaborate chicken coop out back but that wouldn't be very warm right now.

"Trevor installed a heater in the henhouse a couple of months ago. Those chickens are extremely pampered, too." She shrugged. "If my critters are happy, I'm happy."

Luke chuckled. "I can see that. And the chicken craze is spreading. Trevor said Olivia wants some and Badger does, too, once he's settled somewhere."

"I've never baked with freshly laid eggs." Abigail picked up her bowl of stew. "I wonder how much difference that would make."

"You could try it this spring," Kendra said. "If everyone gets chickens, we'll be up to our eyeballs in eggs."

"Then I'll plan on it." She paused. "You know, two weeks ago, I wouldn't have said that. Instead I'd be wondering if I'd still be in operation this spring." She smiled at Luke. "But things are looking up."

Oh, man, did he love the sparkle in her eyes. "They sure are. You should tell Kendra about the new coffee menu. That's exciting."

"You're doing something new with coffee?"

"We will be by Thursday morning." Abigail laid out the plans for Pie in the Sky's newest offering.

As she talked, Kendra's expression grew more animated. "That's brilliant," she said when Abigail finished. "Just what you need."

"Luke's idea."

"Good one, Luke." Kendra gave him a thumbs-up.

"Thanks."

"And the Whine and Cheese Club will want to support it. We all love interesting beverages."

"That would be lovely," Abigail said. "I'll be happy to see all of you whenever you can come by."

"I was thinking about something a little more proactive than just coming by, but I'll need your permission before we spring into action."

"Action?" Abigail looked bewildered. "What kind of action?"

"Not sure yet. I'm making this up on the fly. What time do you open?"

"Six."

"Hm. Okay. Jo and I can be there, no problem. Judy gets up early, too. Deidre and Christine are the sleepyheads, but we'll roust 'em out."

"I'd be honored to serve the Whine and Cheese Club on our first morning. That would be special. But you don't have to show up at six."

"We wouldn't be there to sit around and drink coffee, although I'm sure we'll gulp down our share." She gazed at Abigail. "What would you think about the five of us taking turns standing out on the sidewalk encouraging people to come in and try the coffee?"

"You mean like a carnival barker?"

"Exactly. In costume or not, your call, but either Judy or Christine has a bullhorn left over from their PTA carnival days. Can't remember who has it, but we used it one year to sell raffle tickets at an ENHS football game."

"You'd go to all that trouble?"

"What trouble? This kind of stunt is how we get our kicks. I just don't want you to be horrified if we make fools of ourselves outside your bakery Thursday morning."

"Of course I wouldn't be horrified! I'd be grateful! But I can't believe you'd take your time and energy for my coffee plan."

"Supporting worthy local endeavors is what we do." She glanced at Luke. "What do you think? Too crazy?"

He grinned. "It'll be a riot. The town loves you guys. Great idea."

"Thank you. Personally, I favor the idea of costumes, maybe with a Valentine theme since it'll be the first of February."

"Valentine costumes." Abigail spooned up a mouthful of stew. "I have no idea what that would look like."

"Me, either," Kendra said. "But the Whine and Cheese Club loves a challenge."

"Good. I need all the help I can get."

Luke couldn't be happier with this new alliance. Abigail had caught the ball and run with it. Now Kendra and her friends were getting into the act. Positive steps in the right direction.

The snow had let up a little by the time they finished lunch. After they worked together on the cleanup, he hugged Kendra goodbye and walked Abigail to her SUV.

Delilah bounded along beside them.

Abigail glanced at her. "Have you finally decided that you have a dog, now?"

"Let's just say I've accepted that I'm the guardian of a dog." He described the flyer incident and his conclusion about the people who'd lost Delilah.

"They don't sound very committed to her. I'm glad you've decided to hang tough if another flyer shows up. Although I don't think it will. Not one in good shape, anyway."

"I agree with you, but still, I—"

Delilah gave a little yip and pranced around, as if she wanted to play.

"I know, I know. I need to get you a Frisbee. Or a tennis ball."

"Or this." Abigail picked up a stick and knocked it against her boot to get the snow off. "Here, Delilah. Fetch!" She threw the stick a good twenty yards away and the dog raced after it.

"Good arm, lady!"

"I used to love doing this with our dogs."

Luke smiled. "I hope you still do, because here she comes, ready for more."

"That's okay. It'll wear her out." She accepted the stick and ruffled the dog's ears. "Good dog. Go get it!" She tossed it so energetically that her hood fell back, exposing her tousled hair.

Good thing he was wearing gloves. The urge to reach over and touch those silky curls nearly overwhelmed him. "But you probably want to get home. This is your free day."

She glanced at him. "And I've loved spending it with you." Her gaze, softened by the muted light of the snow clouds, met his for an instant. Then she returned her focus to the dog. "Hey, Delilah! That's it, bring it back. Good dog!" She threw the stick again.

His chest tightened. "I've loved spending it with you, too."

"That's nice to hear." She kept her attention on Delilah, who came back wearing a snow beard and mustache from burrowing in the snow to get the stick. "Look at you, silly girl! Tired yet? No? Okay, then, fetch!" She drew back her arm and hurled the stick.

"And I'm glad we went on this ride today."

"Me, too. It's been amazing." She took the stick from Delilah. "Aha! You're panting, now, aren't you, doggie? Okay, once more." She made her best throw yet before turning to him. "I can't thank you enough for setting this up. It's been wonderful. Kendra inspires me."

"Me, too."

"Am I right that her parents died when she was young like me?" A stray snowflake landed on her cheek and left a moist spot.

He longed to kiss her there. "That's what I hear." But he wouldn't be satisfied with a kiss on the cheek. Moisture from the snow made her mouth glisten, too, and that was where the real treasure lay.

"She's very kind."

"Yes, she is." In this light, Abigail's eyes were more green than gold. Hypnotized by the warmth in her gaze, he stepped closer.

Her breath caught. "Luke..."

He blinked and moved back. "Sorry."

"Don't be." Her voice blended with the whisper of the pines. "But I should go."

He nodded.

Delilah had other ideas. She dropped the stick at Abigail's feet and looked expectant, tail wagging.

"I have to leave, girl." Abigail picked up the stick and handed it to Luke. "Get him to throw it for you." She stroked the dog's head. "I'll see you soon."

"Saturday after closing, right?" Nearly a full week. "I'll bring her if it's still all right."

"Please bring her. I'd be sad if you didn't."

"She'd be sad, too."

"Listen, do you want to come by for a latte on Thursday?" She opened the driver's door.

"I just might do that. How could I miss seeing the Whine and Cheese Club show?"

She smiled. "Exactly." She started to get in but there was a dog in the way. "Uh-oh. Here we go again."

"Delilah, come."

Reluctantly, the dog returned and stood beside him.

"It's nice to be wanted."

He glanced at Abigail. "Don't ever doubt it."

She sucked in a breath.

He held her gaze for a moment before scooping Delilah into his arms and moving away from the SUV. "See you Thursday."

"Looking forward to it." She slid behind the wheel, quickly closed the door and was on her way.

Luke held onto Delilah until the SUV disappeared around a curve in the road. He didn't trust her not to run after it. "You really like her, don't you, pup?"

Delilah whined.

"Yeah, well, so do I, dog." He let out a breath and put her down. "So do I." He picked up the stick at his feet. "Here you go, girl." Going into a full windup, he tossed the stick a respectable distance. "Fetch!"

Delilah sat looking at him as if he was one doughnut shy of a dozen.

He laughed. "Or don't."

14

Abigail anticipated a busy morning so she asked Yolanda and Doug to show up at five-thirty to prep the shop. Yolanda was right on time, her dark hair tucked into a neat bun, her white blouse and dark slacks crisp and clean. Abigail thanked her for making the effort.

"No problem! This coffee thing is a great idea. I—oh, here comes Doug. Gee, he's only like, two minutes late, which is amazing, considering."

Abigail laughed. "Sure is. Hey, Doug! Thanks for getting here so early."

"You bet." He shrugged out of his coat. His blond hair was wet, his shirt was wrinkled and the hem of his jeans looked as if he'd plowed through snowdrifts on his way to the shop. "I'm excited about this coffee deal. So are my friends. They'll be in."

"That's great. Thanks."

"I can't wait until Ingrid trains me to be a *barista*." He snapped his fingers in the air as if he had castanets. "Love the concept."

Abigail laughed. "Good."

"This is the best job I ever had and it's getting even better."

Yolanda nodded. "I so agree."

"Me, too!" Ingrid called from over by the coffee machine.

A knock came at the front door and Doug glanced toward it. "Holy crap! What's *that*?"

"Has to be one of the Whine and Cheese ladies, but I can't tell which one." She hurried to the door.

Someone stood outside in a red parka, red mittens and red ski pants. The shape was female but the parka's hood covered her hair and she'd drawn big lipstick hearts on each cheek. A giant heart sprouted from the top of her head, secured by a plastic headband jammed over the hood.

Abigail peered at the person's eyes. McGavin blue. "Kendra?"

"Yes, ma'am!"

"Great outfit."

"Isn't it? I would've sewn white lace on the parka but it's not mine. I borrowed it from Luke's mom."

"I've seen Virginia in that."

"Me, too, which is why I thought to ask if I could borrow it. And the pants." She glanced back toward the street. "Let me get the others. They didn't want to climb out until the door was open. Wusses." She beckoned to the occupants of a white van with a Wild Creek Ranch logo on the door.

The van door slid back and four women carefully eased out. Three of them wore pink coffee cups with holes cut out for their arms, legs, and faces.

Once they came inside and the staff gathered to admire the costumes, Kendra explained that Judy was small, Deidre was medium and Christine was large. The cups bore sayings like *I love you a latte* and *Espresso your feelings.*

Jo was a giant coffee bean covered in lacy valentines and the slogan *I've always bean yours.*

Doug grinned. "Awesome creativity. You ladies are cool."

"Wonderful costumes," Yolanda said. "But they don't look very warm."

"Never fear," Deidre said. "We have on thermal underwear."

"And I have a hat." Judy pulled on one with earflaps. She'd attached a cardboard disk to the top and piled it with cotton. "Whipped cream."

"Not bad," Deidre said, "but I have *steam.*" The white crepe paper streamers attached to her knit hat came alive and danced in the air above her head.

Judy stared at the fluttering streamers. "How'd you do that?"

"Professional secret."

"Now I feel lame," Christine said. "I didn't embellish the top of my cup."

"Hang on, hang on," Ingrid said. "We still have the white packing paper this beauteous coffee machine was shipped in. Let me get it." She came back with an armful of the wrinkled paper and stapled it around the rim of Christine's cup. "There you go. Foam."

"Excellent. Thanks."

The bell on the front door jingled and Ellie Mae Stockton, the eighty-something clerk from Pills and Pop walked in. "What in the name of all that's holy is going on here?"

"Hi, Ellie Mae." Abigail smiled at her. "These lovely ladies have offered to take turns standing on the sidewalk with a bullhorn to bring in customers."

Ellie Mae glanced around. "Damn, wish I'd known you were doing that. I could've rigged up some outfit or other. And there's nothing I like better than using a bullhorn. Takes me back."

Doug perked up. "Yeah? To what?"

"Crowd control in Hollywood, sonny boy. Loved that job. The idea is to keep a large crowd from turning into an unruly mob. Once that happens, it's almost impossible to restore order."

"We don't want an unruly mob," Deidre said. "Any tips?"

"You won't have an unruly mob in Eagles Nest. Folks around here don't panic easily. But I would love to get my hands on that bullhorn."

"Then you should kick this thing off." Christine handed it to her. "It's six o'clock. Let's rock and roll!"

"Yee-haw!" Ellie Mae took the bullhorn and headed outside. In seconds, she was back. "I forgot to ask. What am I supposed to say, Abigail?"

"Just sell the product. Things like Wake up your taste buds! Tired of the same old grind? Hankering for a better morning joe? One sip and you'll be hooked! Like that."

Ellie Mae nodded. "How about Get your butt in here or you'll regret it?"

Doug snorted.

"That works, too." She walked over and laid her hand on Ellie Mae's arm. "You have the bullhorn. Use it as you see fit."

"Oh, boy." Ellie Mae grinned. "This'll be fun. Eagles Nest, here I come!" She sailed out the door.

Abigail stared after her. "I hope turning her loose wasn't a mistake."

Kendra started to laugh. "You already have a shop full of middle-aged women in gonzo costumes. How much crazier can it get?"

Brakes screeched outside, followed by a shouting match. One of the participants sounded like Ellie Mae.

Barreling out the door, Abigail found her in the street nose-to-nose with an elderly man. His fifties Chevy sat there, engine idling and driver's door standing open.

"I don't care how great the coffee is, Ellie Mae!" the man yelled. "You can't stand in the middle of the street hollering at folks!"

"He's right, Ellie Mae." Abigail put her arm around the woman's shoulders. "You'll have to stay on the sidewalk." She glanced at the irate driver. "Sorry, sir."

The man muttered something under his breath and got back in his car.

"He should have paid attention when I hailed him on the bullhorn," Ellie Mae said. "He ignored me. Didn't turn his head or wave. No acknowledgment whatsoever. And we used to date, too. That stuck in my craw."

"I can tell." Abigail gave her a squeeze. "Promise me you'll stay on the sidewalk, okay?"

She sighed. "I will, but it won't be as much fun."

"Want to trade off with somebody? I'm sure Kendra or Deidre would—"

"No, I want to stay out here for a bit. It might not be as much fun, but it'll still be fun."

"Okay then." Shivering, she hurried back inside where everyone was peering out the window watching the action. "She's promised to stay out of the street."

"Good," Kendra said. "But I can't imagine what made her think she could go out there in the first place."

"An old flame came by and ignored her when she called to him on the bullhorn."

Doug just about killed himself laughing until Yolanda reminded him they had work to do and hauled him back behind the counter to get started.

"I understand why she'd be upset," Deidre said. "But we're here to help the cause, not fight with old lovers."

Kendra gave her a light punch on the arm. "So we can count on you to stay out of the street if one of your old lovers ignores you?"

"Ha! They wouldn't dare. But what should we do while Ellie Mae's out there flagging down customers?"

"Drink coffee?" Ingrid stood by her precious machine looking eager.

Kendra slapped her forehead and almost dislodged her giant heart. "Duh! Yes, please!"

"I might take my coffee for a stroll," Deidre said. "These thermals are heating up my girls."

"Mine, too," Christine said. "Since Ellie Mae has the bullhorn, what if the rest of us walk around town drinking coffee and spreading the word?"

"I'm so videoing that." Kendra brought out her phone. "It's not every day you see three pink coffee cups parading down Main Street."

* * *

Luke got to see the whole show, although he didn't stop at Pie in the Sky. He had Delilah in the truck and the bakery was a zoo. That was great, though. A line out the door, Ellie Mae Stockton wielding the bullhorn like a film director, and three coffee cups sashaying up and down Main Street accompanied by a giant coffee bean.

He figured Kendra was the one wearing the big heart over her head and taking the video. That red parka and ski pants looked familiar. Either she had the exact same set or his mom had loaned out hers.

He had an early appointment with the owner of the feed store. For years, the guy had kept track of inventory old school and was ready to computerize. He didn't mind if Luke brought Delilah to the meeting.

That was convenient, because Kendra wasn't available to dog-sit this morning. Luke didn't want to take advantage of her generous nature, either. Fortunately, most of his clients were fine with him bringing Delilah. Some seemed happier to see the dog than they were to see him.

The meeting went long, nearly two hours. When it was over, the mob scene at Pie in the Sky had calmed considerably. The Whine and Cheese ladies had left and there was no line outside.

Luke figured he could stop by and take Delilah in without causing a problem. He even found a parking space in front. Leaving his hat on the dash, he clipped the leash on Delilah's collar and made sure she didn't step in any puddles before he took her inside.

The bakery was still humming with activity. This was his first glimpse of the two younger employees, Yolanda and Doug. They were clearly earning their wages today. They appeared tired but happy.

Ingrid looked completely exhausted, but she gave him a bright smile when he came in. "There's the man of the hour!"

"Oh, I'm not—"

"The heck you aren't. If you hadn't suggested specialty coffee, we wouldn't have *this*." She swept a hand toward the coffee machine like a game show host showing off a prize.

"It's a beauty."

"Tell me about it! Performs like a champ, too. Want anything?"

"I—"

"Here you go, Ingrid." Yolanda handed her three paperboard cups. "Two medium peppermint lattes and a double shot espresso." Then she glanced at Luke and smiled. "Welcome to Pie in the Sky. Can I get something for you?"

"Thanks," Luke said. "Maybe later. I'm here to see Abigail."

"She's in her office taking a break. I can go tell her you're—"

"That's okay. I'll just go back."

"But—"

"It's okay, Yolanda," Ingrid said. "This is Luke, the business manager who's helping Abigail."

"*Oh.* Pleased to meet you. Sure. Go on back. Although I'm not sure about your dog..."

"Oh, right." Delilah had become such a part of him that he sometimes forgot that she couldn't go everywhere he did. Taking her through the kitchen would break health department rules. "I'll put her in the truck for a few minutes."

He turned around and there was his mother. Lately he'd noticed how much Hayley was like her—blond, slender and vivacious. Whereas he took after his dad, which meant he could look forward to a receding hairline and a highly developed sense of humor. He'd take it.

"Hey, Mom! Here to get coffee?"

She smiled at him. "Yes, I am. But I overheard what you said about putting Delilah in the truck. It's chilly out there."

"I know, but—"

"Why don't I take charge of her while you go see your client?"

Client. It was the right word but sounded wrong. Abigail was so much more. "That would be great." He handed her the leash. "Was that your red parka and ski pants on Kendra this morning?"

"Sure was. I missed seeing how everyone looked, though. I had a consultation with my contractor."

"Those ladies were amazing. And they brought in tons of business."

"That's great!"

"How's the barn coming along?"

"It's going to be fabulous. But I'll tell you about it later. Go ahead and have your business discussion. Delilah and I will wait here."

"I won't be long. Just want to check to see how she's doing and what the receipts look like from this morning." He hoped that sounded official and businesslike. He had no intention of looking at receipts. Mostly he wanted to see Abigail's happy smile.

"Take your time. I'm in no rush."

"Thanks, Mom." He walked through the kitchen and tapped on the office door. "It's Luke."

"Luke!" She flung the door open. "Did you drive by? Did you see the line?"

"I did." He couldn't help grinning. "I saw it all, the coffee cups, the giant coffee bean, Ellie Mae—"

"I know! It was epic!" Her gaze dropped. "Where's Delilah?"

"Couldn't bring her through the kitchen."

"Oh, right."

"My mom happened to show up. She has Delilah up front. Listen, there's something I want to discuss, if I can come in."

"Of course!"

He walked through the door and closed it behind him. "You did great!" And he swept her up in a hug.

She didn't seem to mind. She gazed up at him, eyes sparkling. "*We* did great. All of us, you included."

Now that he had her in his arms, he hated to let go. She looked so pretty, flushed and proud of herself.

Her breathing grew shallow. "We probably shouldn't be doing this."

"Probably not. Looks like I'm going to, anyway." Lowering his head, he captured those smiling lips. Ah, so sweet. Shouldn't stay long...but he lingered and she let him.

He'd never held her like this, cushioned against her soft breasts while exploring her warm and tasty mouth. His body warmed, especially the part below his belt. The kiss was going great until she braced her palms against his chest and pushed gently.

He lifted his head a fraction. "Don't make me stop yet. You taste delicious."

"Chocolate strawberry tart."

"Baker ladies are awesome." He nibbled on her lower lip.

"Your mom's out there holding your dog."

That doused his fire in no time. With a sigh, he let her go and backed toward the door. "See you Saturday, right?"

"That's the plan. Luke, wait. You—"

"I need to go before I grab you again."

"Yes, but—"

"See you Saturday." He left the office and walked to the front of the shop to retrieve Delilah. The dog was enjoying herself. She sat regally beside his mother and allowed herself to be admired and petted by anyone who happened by.

"Ah, there you are," his mother said. "She's been a very good dog."

"Glad to hear it. Thank you for hanging onto her for me."

"You're welcome." She peered at him. "Come over here for a minute."

"What?"

She took a tissue out of her pocket. "Hold still." She dabbed at his mouth. "Lipstick."

His gaze met hers.

"You can't fool your mother. I knew you weren't going in there to discuss receipts. You had that look in your eye."

15

The coffee business continued to be brisk through Saturday afternoon, and most customers wanted a bakery item to go with their brew. The shop ran up some impressive sales numbers. Abigail hoped that success would offset the disorganized state of her records when Luke arrived to delve into them today.

Since their first meeting she'd kept better track. She'd bought some stacking trays and cobbled together a crude filing system for the past two weeks' worth of receipts. Prior to that, though...

It was only paperwork, right? The important thing was cash flow, and it was flowing faster than an open spigot on the new coffee machine.

A knot of anxiety tightened in her stomach, though. She liked Luke and didn't want him to think she was an idiot, especially because he liked her back. His kiss on Thursday had left no doubt.

Would he have kissing on his mind this afternoon? Probably not after she brought out that cardboard box bulging from what she'd stuffed in there since last February.

As four o'clock approached, she and Ingrid were the only ones left in the shop. She'd sent Yolanda and Doug home after praising their dedication. While she closed out the register, Ingrid cleaned her new toy in preparation for shutting it down for the weekend.

"I love this darned thing. So do Yolanda and Doug. They're catching on quick, especially Doug." She polished the brushed chrome surfaces. "I'm so glad you got it."

"It's done a job for us. I had no clue the population of Eagles Nest was so eager for designer coffee."

"Me, either. Otherwise I would have suggested it. I figured most folks in cowboy country liked their coffee strong and black."

"Maybe that's why espressos are outselling lattes. Those rough, tough cowboys discovered the miracle of a double shot."

"Speaking of cowboys, Luke just drove up."

She glanced out the front window. "Yep." And she wasn't ready to face him alone. "Do you have anywhere you need to be right now?"

"Not really. Why?"

"It's been a while since we took out the shelves in the display case and cleaned in the corners."

"I thought Yolanda and Doug did a pretty good job yesterday afternoon."

"They cleaned the case? Where was I?"

"In your office sorting receipts. And muttering."

She swallowed. "I'm so nervous about this meeting, Ingrid. My records are a hot mess."

"He's a nice guy. He's not going to yell at you. But I'll stay if you need me to. I'll find something to keep me busy."

"No, don't stay. I'll handle this."

"Sure you will." Ingrid gave her an encouraging smile. "But if you need backup, text me and I'll come running." Her gaze flicked toward the door as it opened. "Hi, Luke! I see you brought your partner along."

"Yes, ma'am." He took off his hat and laid it on a nearby table. "She was so excited when she figured out where we were going."

"That's nice to hear." Abigail gave him a quick smile as she walked around the counter. "How's my favorite doggie?" She buried her fingers in Delilah's luxurious ruff. The dog wouldn't care if her paperwork was orderly.

"Can I give her a treat?" Ingrid asked. "Abigail bought dog biscuits."

"One's okay." He put down his laptop case and unhooked the leash from Delilah's collar. "I was just out at Wild Creek Ranch and Kendra has biscuits for her, too. Don't want to spoil her."

"I understand," Ingrid said. "But that face just makes you want to give her stuff. She's so cute."

"Yeah, she is." Abigail stepped back as Ingrid came over with the biscuit. "And so happy." Petting Delilah had improved her mood considerably.

"But I want her to be mannerly, too." He unbuttoned his jacket, took it off and laid it over a chair. "How about if you tell her to sit before you give it to her?"

Ingrid held the biscuit up. "Delilah, sit."

The dog's haunches dropped instantly.

"Good dog!" Ingrid gave her the biscuit. "She minds so well, Luke."

"She does most of the time. But once in a while...let's just say she's got a mind of her own."

Ingrid laughed. "An independent female. I like that. Well, I'm off. Errands to run before the weather changes." She peered out the window. "Assuming it does. Think it's gonna snow?"

"Depends on which forecaster you listen to," Luke said. "Just now on the radio they said it would pass us by."

"I hope so. See you two later!"

"'Bye, Ingrid!" Abigail turned to Luke. "I take it no other lost dog flyers have shown up?"

"No." He heaved a sigh and glanced toward the corner where Delilah had curled up the last time he was here. "You put out water for her. Thanks."

"And bought dog treats. I hope that's okay."

"Ah, why not? Like Ingrid said, nobody can resist that face." He glanced down at the dog. "Okay, girl, go lie down." He pointed toward the corner with the water dish.

She headed right to it, circled and flopped down.

"Ingrid's right. She really does mind."

He chuckled. "Except when she doesn't want you to leave. And after you did, she refused to play fetch."

"Really? That surprises me."

"I think she was mad at me because I let you go."

"Nah. She was just tired."

"If she was, that would be a first. There's no *off* switch on that dog." He smiled as he said it.

"You like that about her, don't you?"

"I do. I can't imagine anyone feeling down when they're around Delilah. She's like a furry bundle of optimism. Listen, before I forget, would you like to go for another ride tomorrow?"

"I'd love to."

"If that storm hits, we'll have to cancel, but I'm going with what the guy on the radio said. It'll pass us by."

"Then let's plan on it." She liked talking about the dog and a potential horseback ride. These were cheerful topics. Non-threatening topics.

"Great." He rubbed his hands together. "Let's dive into those records. I'm ready to power through them."

"Right! But wouldn't you like some coffee, first? I'm not going to mess up Ingrid's precious machine, but the old model still works."

"Maybe later, after we've made some progress."

"Okay, some cookies, then. I held back some oatmeal raisin ones just for this occasion." Ha. Bribes R Us.

"That sounds great, but let's get some work done and then take a break."

"All right." The knot in her stomach was back. "I thought we'd start with the past two weeks. Those are better organized than—"

"I'd rather see it all at once. That way I can get a better idea of what we're looking at. Is everything in your office?"

"It's...um...yes."

"Would you rather work in there or out here?"

"Out here. We'd be crowded in that small office. I'll bring the box out here where there's more room to spread out."

He brightened. "A file box?"

"Not quite. I got a shipment of napkins in it."

"Oh." He started toward the office. "I'll bring it out. It's probably heavy."

"Not really, and I'm familiar with it." She hurried to get in front of him and backed toward the office. "Better let me get it. The bottom's...we had a small leak...never mind. I'll be right back." She made a shooing motion. "You can go sit down."

"Thanks, but I'll stay here." He crossed his arms.

"Okay." The box was on the floor. She'd thrown a holiday tablecloth over it so she didn't have to look at it every day. But knowing what was under there was about as bad as staring at the contents.

Whipping off the tablecloth decorated with poinsettias, she crouched down and shoved her hands under the box. Still a little damp. A pipe in the wall had sprung a leak in December.

Luckily when she lifted the box, it held together. But it was heavier than she remembered and she staggered a little. Once she was balanced, she walked out of the office.

Luke's eyes widened. "That's...that's..."

"My paperwork. Except for the last couple of weeks." She carried it through the kitchen. The bottom started to give way as she rounded the counter. Moving faster, she made it to one of the bistro tables, set the box down with a thud and turned around.

Luke stood several feet away, his gaze alternating between her and the box. "I'm...a little surprised."

Heat rose in her cheeks. "I knew you wouldn't like it."

"It's not a matter of liking or not liking. But sorting through all that could take hours. Or days."

"How much do you charge per hour? It occurs to me we should have discussed that before I—"

"We didn't talk about it because I decided early on you couldn't afford my hourly charge."

"You're not doing it for free. I won't accept that."

"I'm not doing it for free. But there's no point in pretending you're the same as every other client."

His gaze strayed to the box again and she bristled. "Then what are you going to charge me? I need to know."

"Nothing until your business is out of the woods."

"And when it is? Then what?"

"We'll decide together what my services were worth to you. Then we'll set up a payment plan that's not too arduous."

"I've never heard of anyone doing that."

"I don't plan to make it a habit, but setting my own fee structure is one of the benefits of being self-employed." He glanced at the box again. "Is there any order to what's in there?"

"Of course! The oldest stuff is on the bottom." Yeah, she was defensive. Not good.

He massaged the back of his neck. "Judging from the water line on that box, the items on the bottom might not be viable anymore."

"I thought of that. I decided letting it sit and dry on its own was the best plan. If I tried taking things out, I might make it worse."

"Really?"

"No, not really." She hated this. Hated it with the heat of a supernova. "I knew that once I started digging into that box, I'd have to do something with all of it."

"Like what?"

She waved a hand in the air. "Organize it. File it. Computerize it." *Douse it with lighter fluid and throw a match on it.*

"Why didn't you?"

"I meant to. Each month I'd promise myself I'd take a Sunday afternoon and sort through everything. Then I'd come to the last Sunday of the month and put it off again."

"I see."

"Look, if this is too big a challenge for you, don't feel you have to—"

"I'm not intimidated."

"Well I am!"

"I can see that. But I can help you. We'll develop a system to get your paperwork under control."

"But you said it would take hours, maybe days. I can't put that kind of demand on your time. It's not fair."

He scrubbed a hand over his face. "Look, you're not demanding anything, okay? Just the opposite. You're trying to get rid of me."

"Only because—"

"You're embarrassed."

"Am not." But the heat in her cheeks contradicted her.

"It's okay, Abigail. You're not the first person to get overwhelmed by paperwork. Let me help. We can do this."

"How? If it could take days, you probably need a place to leave stacks of paper. This isn't it."

"True. What about your apartment? Would that work?"

"Uh, maybe." Her apartment? That would bring the chaos up close and personal. She'd hoped to avoid that. It would also bring him into her private space. "If we use my apartment, we'd have to get that box up a steep flight of stairs and the bottom's compromised."

"I hate when that happens."

She glanced at him. He was smiling. "You find this amusing?"

"Yes, ma'am, I do."

"Well, I don't." She looked at the sagging napkin carton. She hadn't paid quarterly taxes, either. If, on top of that, she sent in a return made up of guestimates, she could get audited. "What would happen if I took that box to the Feds? Would they be amused?"

Laughter sparkled in his eyes. "I can't say. But you'd have to reinforce it first."

"Definitely." She met his gaze. "I'm thinking some of that fancy duct tape. The kind with peacock feathers on it."

"I'd go with the sock monkey design, but that's just me."

She laughed. Couldn't help it. "You're right. This is effing hilarious."

"Told you." He reached for his jacket and put it on. "Let's get this disreputable box up to your apartment."

16

At least he'd changed the mood. And Abigail hadn't bailed on him.

For the trip upstairs, Abigail put herself in charge of Delilah and the water bowl. He followed with the box. He shoved one arm under the soggy bottom and the other around the girth of the thing. *Please hold, dammit.*

By some miracle, it did. At the top of the stairs, Abigail headed for the first door on the left. Good. The box might not make it the length of the hall. She didn't use a key to get in, which surprised him.

"You don't lock your door?"

"None of us do. Just the downstairs door. We like having access to each other's rooms."

"So it's like college."

"Pretty much."

"Interesting." He followed her into the apartment and didn't bother to close the door. For all he knew she left it open. "Where should I put this?"

"The table in my dining nook." She flipped on lights as she moved through the apartment followed closely by Delilah. "I'll get the candlesticks out of the way. You can use the couch and the coffee table as you take things out of the box."

He put the box on the table and surveyed the area. Neat and tidy, just like the bakery. A comfortable-looking couch, a few colorful throw pillows and a crocheted afghan over the back. Magazines in a basket, books stacked on a side table, a green plant of some kind on the coffee table. No clutter. Evidently shoving receipts into a shipping carton was an outlier in an otherwise organized life.

Her living room was small but better than the postage stamp of an office downstairs. The dining table would be a good base of operations. "How do you feel about not having use of your living and dining room for a few days?"

She answered him from the kitchen, where she'd gone with Delilah, probably to fill the pup's water bowl. "It's better than losing my business."

"Yes. Yes, it is."

"Hey, guys!" Ingrid appeared in the open doorway, a loaded sack of groceries in each arm. "Looks like you moved the party up here."

"More room to sort things," Luke said. "You need help with those?" Delilah joined him at the door, tail wagging.

"Hi, doggie! I'm fine, Luke, but thanks. The relevant question is, do you two need anything?"

Abigail came out of the kitchen. "I don't think so, but thanks for offering."

"No problem. Just FYI, the wind just whipped up. When I got out of the car it was still, but now it's blowing like a banshee out there."

"Appreciate the heads up." Luke silently thanked Mother Nature for holding off on the wind until he'd carried the box from the bakery to the apartment.

"You're welcome. I doubt there will be any takeout delivery tonight but I bought a couple of frozen lasagna meals, the big size. You're welcome to one if you're going to work through dinner."

Abigail glanced at him. "Are you planning to?"

Luke hadn't gone that far in his thinking. Operating in this intimate space with Abigail might pose a challenge if they got cozy over a meal. "Probably not. For one thing, Delilah needs to be fed."

"I have some leftover chicken," Abigail said. "She could have that."

"Thanks, but I really should take her home."

"All righty," Ingrid said. "Let me know if that changes. Roxanne and I are baking the lasagna and watching *The Magnificent Seven*." She glanced at Abigail. "Come by when you and Luke are finished for the night."

"I will. Save me some."

"Sure thing. 'Bye." She turned and walked down the hall.

"I can see how this would be fun, living here." Luke gestured toward the door. "Should I close it? Or do you just leave it open?"

She laughed. "That would be a little too much togetherness. You can close it."

"Okay." The simple act of closing the door shouldn't have affected him. It did. With the door closed he was truly alone with Abigail and all the possibilities that presented.

Except she didn't lock that door, did she? Ingrid and Roxanne felt free to walk in anytime they wanted to. Yet they might not if they knew he was here.

Didn't matter. He had one job—organizing the contents of that damned box. The sooner he got to it, the better. "I could make use of that coffee table. Do you mind if I move the plant?"

"Not at all. I'll put it in the kitchen." She scooped it up and left.

He took off his coat and laid it over the arm of the couch. Then he put his hat on top of it.

"Want that coffee and a plate of cookies, now?"

He turned. Abigail stood in the kitchen doorway smiling. His breath caught. For one wild moment, he was the guy living with her, the guy who had the right to share this space with her and follow her down the hall to the bedroom at the end of each day. Longing swept through him.

Clearing his throat, he smiled back. "That would be terrific."

"Then I'll put on the pot." She returned to the pocket-sized kitchen.

Whew. Almost hijacked by his fantasies. Rolling back his sleeves, he stepped over to the box and pulled out a stack of papers from the top. Delilah appeared at his side, and when he started toward the coffee table she tried to maneuver him toward the kitchen, instead.

"Sorry, girl. I'm not going in there." Small space, close quarters. Nope. "You'll have to work on Abigail."

Delilah trotted away, and moments later Abigail called to him. "Luke, your dog's herding me!"

He smiled. "Tell her no."

"I've tried. She won't listen."

"Oh." Because he'd told her to go work on Abigail. He'd given her a direct command and she was determined to follow orders. "Be right there." He put down the stack of papers and went as far as the kitchen doorway.

Abigail stood with her hands on her hips. "I was planning to bring you a cup of coffee and a plate of cookies, but evidently I wasn't doing it fast enough to suit her."

"I'll just take it, then." He stepped in far enough to grab his coffee. Next to it sat a plate piled with cookies. "Are those all for me?"

"Not unless you can eat that many. I thought I'd sit at the table and we'd share."

"Great. Delilah will like that." And he'd keep his attention firmly on the work. And put her to work, too, for that matter. He carried the plate into the dining nook.

Abigail followed with her coffee and a couple of napkins. "Going through this box might be a relief, in a way."

"Like breaking off a bad relationship."

"Yeah, like that. This box and I have been involved in a very toxic relationship."

He put down his coffee. "Once we get everything out of it, we'll put it in the dumpster."

"I'm in favor of a ritual burning, but I don't have a safe place to do it."

"I do." He reached in the box for another stack.

"That's right, you do! I could cut it up and burn it at your place. That would be awesome."

"Then plan on it." And he couldn't wait for that day, or evening, as the case might be. This situation was causing her stress and he wanted it over.

He handed her the stack of papers. "I'm turning this stack over to you. Separate them out by date."

"I bet most of your clients have their paperwork organized." Her voice had a touch of anxiety.

"No worries. Once we set up a good filing system, yours will be, too." He'd handled situations like hers before, although not quite this extreme. Putting her at ease was part of the job. "Sorting it out now is no big deal, though."

"Okay." She started going through the stack while munching on a cookie.

He should get busy, too. Instead he watched every bite of cookie disappear into her mouth. Her lush, kissable mouth.

Enough. He focused on his work. Moments later, a soft whine broke his concentration. Delilah sat by the kitchen door looking expectant.

Abigail glanced at the dog. "I think she's hungry. What time do you usually feed her?"

He checked the clock on her living room wall. "Sometime between now and six. Did you say you had some leftover chicken?"

"I sure do!" She hopped up. "Come on, Delilah! Din-din!"

The dog left without a backward glance in his direction. Abigail returned a few minutes later, shaking her head. "She wouldn't eat until I told her it was okay."

He'd gotten so used to Delilah's habit that he didn't think about it anymore. "Someone trained her well." Which didn't match with the bare-bones flyer and lack of follow-up. The uncertainty in those contradictions kept gnawing at him.

They worked steadily without talking. He did his best to concentrate, but Abigail kept making little noises of frustration as she sorted receipts—a fretful sigh, an impatient exhale, a murmured swear word. Signs of stress.

He'd polished off more than half the plate of cookies, but as far as he could tell, she'd only had one. Instead of eating she was frowning, her full lips pressed together in a grim line. Time to quit so she could get her happy face back.

He put his stack of unsorted papers back in the box. "That's enough for tonight."

Lifting her head, she blinked. "But you said an hour and it's only been—"

"I know, but you've put in a long day. I'll bet the job won't be as tough after you've had some rest."

Relief brightened her expression. "I could keep going, but if you're ready to quit, I won't argue."

"Good. We'll leave everything as is." He shoved back his chair and stood. Delilah roused herself from where she'd been snoozing in the corner and sauntered over to stand beside him.

"So I should just leave this here?" She gestured to the receipts she'd been sorting.

"If they haven't been sorted, they can go in the box for now." He tucked them in on top.

"That's fine. I won't touch anything."

That made him smile. She probably wouldn't look at it, either. The job would take longer if they spaced it out over several days, but that was better than causing her major stress. "Are you up for spending another hour on it after our ride tomorrow?"

"Of course."

"Then Delilah and I will be on our—"

"Let me fix you dinner."

"Weren't you supposed to have lasagna with Ingrid and Roxanne?"

"I can text them. Do you like spaghetti?"

Delilah looked up at Luke and wagged her tail.

"Looks like she's eager to stay." Coincidentally, so was he. "But since you're asking, I love spaghetti." He also loved seeing the light return to her eyes.

"I made a big batch of sauce last weekend. I can have the meal on the table in no time. Fixing you dinner will make me feel better about..." She gestured toward the box. "What I'm putting you through."

"I promise it's not a hardship, but dinner sounds great."

"Okay, then. I'll start the spaghetti."

"I should take Delilah out before we eat, though. Where can I go?"

"The alley beside the bakery would work."

"I've seen it." Putting on his coat, hat and gloves, he took the leash from where he'd hung it on the front doorknob. "Come on, girl." He patted his thigh.

Delilah didn't look excited about leaving the warm apartment or Abigail. She wandered over with a distinct lack of enthusiasm.

"You'll thank me later, pup." He clipped the leash to her collar. "Be back in a few."

Delilah followed him reluctantly out the door and down the stairs.

"We're not leaving, girl. Just taking a break." Cold sliced through his jacket the minute he stepped outside. The wind Ingrid had mentioned had died down, but snow was falling and it had started to pile up.

He'd need to head out after dinner, but sharing a meal with Abigail was the right thing to do. Her reaction to the box of unsorted receipts had taught him that he'd have to tread carefully as he untangled her snarled financial picture. She clearly hated paperwork, but felt terrible about the mess she'd created by avoiding it, too. In her mind, it probably looked like a no-win scenario.

Walking fast, he led Delilah over to the alley. Smart dog that she was, she took care of business in a hurry and they quickly retraced their path.

Warmth and the scent of spaghetti sauce greeted him as he stepped into the entry and locked the door. Climbing the stairs and entering Abigail's fragrant apartment pushed all his happy buttons. She probably had a yummy dessert somewhere in that kitchen, too.

He recited Kendra's advice under his breath as he hung up Delilah's leash. *Follow your instincts.* Shedding his hat and jacket, he walked toward the kitchen.

17

Thank God Luke had decided to take a break. Abigail drained the spaghetti and took pasta bowls out of the cupboard. No two ways about it, working on the receipts was an icky experience, a reminder of her shameful negligence.

But as the kitchen filled with the aroma of her favorite spaghetti sauce and Luke walked back into the apartment with Delilah, her mood took a huge swing upward. She might be lousy at bookkeeping, but she was terrific at feeding people.

"Smells great!" He appeared in the kitchen, his cheeks pink from the cold, his faithful dog right behind him. "What can I do?"

Just stand there and look gorgeous. "Could you make sure the box won't be in the way while we eat? Maybe move it to one side or something."

"I'm on it." He started out of the kitchen and Delilah followed. "By the way, it's snowing."

"Uh-oh. Are you worried about driving home?"

"Not really. I have four-wheel-drive. Besides, I'm not about to miss out on that spaghetti."

"I'll have it ready in a sec." By the time he came back, she'd dished the spaghetti and ladled on the sauce. "Where's Delilah?"

"Curled up in a corner looking happy to be here. She thought I was taking her home."

"But wouldn't that be a good thing? She loves her home."

"She does, but she's also fond of you."

The way he said it gave her shivers of pleasure. "I'm glad. The feeling's mutual." She held up her cheese grinder. "Parmesan?"

"You bet. Classy restaurant you have here."

She covered the pasta with a light layer of cheese. "Thanks. I don't fix dinner often."

"Too busy baking?"

"You've got that right. It's miraculous I had something to give your dog and you."

"Our good luck."

"I was planning to offer you wine." She set down the grinder and grabbed an oven mitt so she could take a cookie sheet of toasted garlic bread out of the oven. "But not if you'll end up driving home in the snow."

"Water's fine for me. And the bread looks awesome."

"We're ready." She spread a cloth napkin in a basket and arranged the bread in it. "If you want to take in the pasta, I'll bring the bread and silverware."

"Before I do that, where did you put those candlesticks that were on the dining table?"

"I tucked them in my pantry. A candlelight dinner is a nice thought, but now that we're tackling that box, I don't want to chance catching it on fire."

"No worries. I moved it off the table."

"Oh?"

He shrugged. "It didn't add a single thing to the ambiance."

"You're a very perceptive guy." She met his gaze and smiled. "You moved that box for my sake, didn't you?"

"Whenever you look at it your jaw clenches."

He was right, but she was touched that he'd noticed. "I appreciate the effort. I promise to get better at this reconciling stuff."

"You're doing fine." His expression was kind. "It'll get easier."

"You know what? I believe you. I'll get the candlesticks and candles. And placemats. Might as well do this right."

What a difference those added touches made. Removing the box would have been enough to change the dynamic, but candlelight, colorful placemats and cloth napkins turned the impromptu meal into an occasion.

He held her chair before taking his seat across from her. "I have another suggestion."

"Keep 'em coming. They've worked great for me so far."

"Let's talk about something besides business."

"I'm all for that." She spread her napkin in her lap and picked up her fork. "I've been wanting to ask you something for weeks."

"Fire away." He expertly twirled the pasta around his fork and popped it in his mouth. "Mm."

"My mom's recipe."

He chewed and swallowed. "It's really good." He gathered another forkful. "So what's your big question?"

"That conversation we had the night you rescued Delilah. You seemed worried about whether your mom had mentioned that you were single. What was that all about?"

He took a slice of garlic bread. "First let me say that I love my mom. She's amazing and she and my dad are awesome parents."

"Disclaimer duly noted."

He looked amused. "Much as I love my mother, I was afraid she'd been up to her old tricks."

"Like what?" She tucked into her spaghetti. It always tasted good, but sharing it with Luke made it even more delicious.

"Matchmaking, specifically for her kids."

"It's a time-honored tradition, Luke. Moms were probably lining up suitable mates for their children in the Stone Age."

"That may be, but my mother has taken it to a new level. Hayley got the worst of it. She was so frustrated by Mom's constant parade of bachelors every Christmas holiday that she introduced Badger as her pretend fiancé."

"So *that's* what was going on. I picked up on some rumors but I never got the whole story."

"It turned into a Bennett family drama. Mom was devastated to discover that she was the cause of the fake fiancé caper and she promised to quit trying to marry us off."

"But Badger and Hayley are a couple, right?"

"A couple, yes. While pretending to be in love, they fell in love for real. But they're not engaged. Hayley wants to make sure they know each other really well first."

"That's smart."

"I think so, too. As to the night you and I met at the GG, you said Mom had been talking about me and alarm bells went off."

"I can see how they would."

"I'm sure she's trying to keep hands off, but it's tough for her. She's happily married and thinks her kids should be, too." He reached for another piece of bread. "I was hoping to keep our relationship on the down-low, but I blew that program on Thursday."

"Because your mom noticed the lipstick?"

He gave her a sheepish smile. "Yes, ma'am."

"Oh, Luke." She couldn't help laughing. "I tried to say something, but you—"

"Ran out like my hair was on fire. I'm aware of that. Totally did it to myself." His gaze warmed. "Worth it, though."

Her heart rate kicked up several notches. "She would have found out, eventually. We went to the GG together. It's a small town. People notice things."

"True. I'm still getting used to that."

"I'm surprised none of my customers have mentioned seeing me having dinner with you."

"Would they?"

"If they were there and noticed, definitely. I'm sure it's common knowledge that I haven't dated anyone since I moved here."

"Seriously?" He put down his fork and glanced at her. "Nobody?"

"I've been asked a few times, but it just seemed too complicated. I go to bed at eight and get up at three. On Sundays, I sleep an extra couple of hours, but I still can't stay up late or I'll be zonked on Monday. That schedule doesn't mesh with the usual dating routine."

"But you went out with me."

"Yes, well..." Her cheeks warmed.

"Which is pretty amazing considering how I bobbled the invitation. I guess you must like me a little."

She smiled. "Just a little bit."

"But I'm still surprised you haven't gone out with anyone. If a guy used his imagination, a lot could happen between four and eight."

Oh, my. Adrenaline pumped through her system, making her giddy. "That's what Ingrid says."

"Good for Ingrid. I knew I liked her."

"She's something else. She got Roxanne and me Christmas condoms..." She clapped her hand over her mouth as heat rushed to her face.

He cracked up. "Christmas condoms?"

"I can't believe I just told you that."

"Okay, now I have to know. Are they red and green? Red and white striped like a candy cane? Decorated with pictures of snowmen?" He wiped tears of laughter from his eyes.

"No, no! They're just regular ones." His laughter was infectious.

"So she just called them Christmas condoms when she gave them to you."

"Oh, she did more than that. She wrapped them individually in holiday paper and added little tags that said stuff."

His eyes gleamed. "Like what?"

"Let me think." She pushed aside her empty pasta bowl. "Things like, *Ring in the New Year, Spread Good Cheer, Be Joyful and Triumphant.* Like that."

"That's hilarious. I'll have a tough time keeping a straight face next time I see her."

"Do your best, please. I can't imagine what made me tell you."

The laughter faded from his expression to be replaced by something much hotter. "I can. I'll bet you can, too, if you think about it."

"Oh, no. Don't look at me like that. I'm not trying to start something. I'm really not." Her heartbeat was out of control. "It's snowing. You need to get home before the roads get bad."

"If I'd been worried about the roads, I wouldn't have stayed for dinner."

That rang true. He'd dismissed the problem in favor of spending time with her. She'd found that dashing. "But you said you'd leave right after."

"I know. At the time, I meant it." He pushed back his chair.

She could barely breathe. "I don't...I don't want you to do anything foolish."

"I won't." He rounded the table and drew her from her chair. "I was raised in snow country. I can deal with it."

Her resistance melted in the heat of his gaze. "I'm sure you can. But the last thing I want is to make life more difficult for you."

"I'll tell you what would be difficult." He pulled her close. "Driving home in a snowstorm and knowing I'd given up a chance to be with you." He held her gaze. "I want to stay, but I haven't asked what you want."

She took a shaky breath. "You. I want you."

_18_

What a rush. Luke's heart raced. _I want you._ Abigail's murmured words, the snowflakes drifting past her window, the promise of what she was willing to share with him—dreams were like this. The good ones, anyway. Any minute he expected to wake up in his own bed, the scent of sawdust in the air from the latest sanding project.

Her hand was soft and warm as she threaded her fingers through his. "Come with me." She led him down a short hall and into a room filled with the glow from a lamp shaped like a cupcake.

Yeah, he was dreaming. That crazy lamp cinched it.

Giving his hand a squeeze, she released it and closed the bedroom door. Then she walked over to the bed. Maybe now she'd vanish into thin air. Instead she threw back the covers and turned, unbuttoning her blouse as she walked back to him.

"Let me." He caught her hands and drew them away from the buttons. He still might wake up. In the meantime, he'd enjoy the heck out of this dream.

She gazed at him, her eyes luminous. "Kiss me, Luke."

"Great idea." Burying his fingers in her mop of silken curls, he tilted her head back. Her lips parted and her eyelashes fluttered down to rest on her smooth cheeks. With a groan, he settled his mouth over hers.

The moment he touched down, the floodgates opened. He poured every bit of his hunger into that kiss, feasting on her lips and using his tongue to gather the sweet nectar of her mouth. He couldn't get enough of this. He might never get enough.

The longer he kissed her, the less he wanted to stop. She seemed in no mood to end it, either. Clutching the back of his head, she opened to him in an invitation that heated his blood and sent it racing south.

He kissed her until his lungs ached and his jeans tightened to the point of pain. Breathing hard, he lifted his head and gulped for air. "I love...kissing you."

Her lashes flicked upward, revealing passion-dark eyes. "Not half as much as I love kissing you."

"It would almost be enough."

"Almost." She leaned into him. "But not quite."

His breath hissed out as she put pressure on his fly. "Easy, Abby."

Her startled gaze met his. "Abby?"

"It seemed right." He searched her expression. "You don't like it?"

Her smile blossomed. "I do when you say it."

"Nobody's ever called you that?"

"I wouldn't let them."

"But you'll let me?" That pleased him.

She nodded and snuggled closer. "In fact, I'll let you do anything you want."

"I hope you mean that." He slipped his hands inside the open collar of her blouse and massaged her shoulders. "Because I have a long list. Might take a while to get through everything."

She took a ragged breath. "Go for it."

"Think I'll start with this." He undid the rest of the buttons on her blouse, tugged it from the waistband of her jeans and took it off.

He couldn't say what happened to her blouse after that. He lost track of it. All his attention was focused on a red lace bra that cupped two helpings of heaven. His cock twitched, suggesting he might want to get on with it, but...so pretty, rising and falling with each breath.

Arching her back, she reached for the hooks, unfastened them and pulled off the lacy garment to unveil the treasures underneath. The view got better and better.

Her nipples responded to his hot gaze by tightening into burgundy peaks. Sliding an arm around her waist, he drew her closer and cradled one of those satin breasts. He was torn between the erotic view of his thumb brushing lazily over that rigid tip and the gleam of sensuality in her eyes as he caressed her.

Drawing her toward the bed, he sat on the edge of the mattress and guided her down so she could straddle his knees. The urge to taste her was so strong his throat hurt. Leaning down, he swiped his tongue over her nipple.

She whimpered. "More."

"Count on it," he murmured against her skin right before he drew that tempting bud into his mouth. The blood roared in his ears as he began to nibble and suck. So good.

She scooted forward until she was tucked against his package. Then she rocked gently. Talk about heaven and hell, pleasure and pain. Combustible friction. They might both come with most of their clothes still on.

He didn't want that. Sliding his hands under her hips, he lifted and turned her, placing her on the bed while he knelt between her thighs.

"Luke..." She was panting and her eyes glittered as she fumbled with his zipper. "Could we—"

"Soon."

"I'm—"

"I know. Let's get you out of these clothes." He abandoned the pleasure of her full breasts so he could pull off her boots.

She helped by unfastening her jeans and wiggling out of both jeans and red satin panties. When she kicked them away, she was...amazing.

Easing her back on the bed, he returned to the sensual playground that was Abby. He massaged and kissed her breasts while she pressed her fingertips into his scalp and arched upward.

The intoxicating scent of aroused woman swirled around him. When he reached between her thighs, she was wet and ready. He scooted down, hooked her knees over his shoulders and gave her the most intimate kiss of all. In seconds, she cried out as an orgasm claimed her and left her quivering.

Nuzzling her damp curls, he stayed with her until she came back to earth. Then he kissed his way to her mouth and propped himself on his elbows so he could gaze into her eyes. Her easy smile of feminine satisfaction was all the reward he needed.

She sighed happily. "Oh, Luke."

"Oh, Abby."

Her smile widened. "I'm going to love having you call me that."

"Good." He pushed away from the bed and began stripping off his clothes. "Because it really suits you when you're naked."

"Speaking of naked, slow down. I want to savor." She moved so she was lying lengthwise on the bed and propped her head on her hand.

He slowed down, not because he was into showing off his body, but because it gave him time to appreciate how beautiful she was lying on a snowy white sheet. "Stretched out like that, you're definitely more Abby than Abigail."

"But not when I'm dressed?"

"Maybe not. But when you started unbuttoning your blouse, you turned into Abby in my mind. That's why it popped out of my mouth."

"So you won't call me that other times?"

"Oh, I'm sure I will. Mostly when I'm imagining you naked."

"Luke!" She started laughing. "I can't have you doing that when other people are around. I'll turn a million shades of red."

"I know. That'll be fun."

"I should dream up a nickname for you. I should..." Her voice trailed off.

"Should what?" He took off his boxers.

"I forgot." She was focused on his privates, specifically his very excited cock.

Her heated gaze stirred him up even more. He approached the bed. "You wanted to give me a nickname. But you can't shorten Luke."

"Wouldn't want to." She glanced up. "Before you bring all that male beauty into bed and I lose my ever-loving mind, I just have to say it. You're magnificent."

"Okay, now I'm blushing."

"It's true. I'm a lucky girl."

"You don't know that, yet." He climbed in beside her. "But if you'll tell me where you stashed the condoms, you'll soon find out."

"In the lamp table drawer."

"Logical." He pulled open the drawer and took them out. He almost asked about the cupcake lamp but decided against it. He didn't want to talk about her crazy taste in lighting. He didn't want to talk at all.

* * *

When Luke turned away to fetch the condoms, Abigail took a steadying breath. She'd expected him to look good. She hadn't expected a body that made her want to fall to her knees in gratitude. Or fall to her knees with a different purpose in mind.

Not this time, though. She longed to make that age-old, basic connection with him. She'd longed for that from the first time they'd danced, from their first kiss.

And now she would have it. He rolled on a condom and moved between her thighs. Balanced on his forearms, his gaze sought hers as he probed once, hands-free. That was confidence.

Her heart pounded. She could barely breathe. The next moment would be…

He pushed deep.

Perfect.

He went very still. Then his chest heaved. "Intense."

"Mm-hm."

"You okay?" His words were strained.

"Mm-hm. You?"

"More than okay." His voice was husky. "Being inside you feels so…"

"Right?"

"Yeah. Like I've been waiting…" He swallowed. "Waiting for this."

"Me, too."

"Ah, Abby." Holding her gaze, he began to move, stroking her with long, sure thrusts.

She picked up his rhythm, rising to meet him, matching him breath for breath. Her core tightened. Soon.

His jaw muscles clenched. Heat poured from his body. "Can you come?"

She dug her fingers into the undulating muscles of his ass. "Yes."

"I can wait." He gasped. "Or not."

"Don't wait." She arched into him as he pumped faster. "I want this, Luke! I want—"

"Abby, oh, God, Abby!" Pressing his mouth against her shoulder to muffle his roar of triumph, he came, bringing her with him.

She clung to him as her world exploded. Held him as he shuddered in her arms. Closed her eyes and thanked her lucky stars that Luke Bennett was in her bed. And even better, in her life.

19

After such cataclysmic lovemaking, Abigail had no interest in leaving this room. Ever. Evidently Luke didn't want to, either. He'd disposed of the condom and climbed right back in bed to cuddle with her.

She gazed into his eyes and smiled at the gleam of satisfaction there. "You look happy."

"I am. You look happy, too."

"I absolutely am. But do you think you should check the weather?"

"No." He leaned down to nuzzle her earlobe. "I don't really care what—" He paused to listen as a muted chorus of *Going to the Chapel* drifted in from the living room. "Oops. My bad. Should have anticipated that. Probably woke up the dog, too." With a sigh, he climbed out of bed, put on his boxers and left the room.

Abigail got up and grabbed her robe from the closet. It didn't take a genius to figure out who was trying to reach him. When she walked into the living room, he was in the process of returning the call. Delilah sat gazing up at him in adoration, her tail thumping the carpet.

He put the phone to his ear. "Hi, Mom! No, I'm not home, but I'm safe and warm, so no worries." He walked to the window and rubbed his fist over it to clear the condensation. Delilah followed.

"Yes, ma'am, she's sitting right here beside me, bright-eyed and bushy-tailed. We sure did get a ton of snow, didn't we?" He motioned Abigail over and stepped back from the window. "Wow. That must be a record or something."

She walked to the window and stood on tiptoe to see through the circle he'd created. While she'd been cavorting with him in the bedroom, Mother Nature had dumped a mountain of snow on Eagles Nest. A symmetrical lump near the building had to be the cab of Luke's truck. He wouldn't be driving it tonight.

She stepped away from the window and glanced at Luke, eyebrows raised.

Giving her a quick shrug, he continued to talk to his mother about the weather. "Really? The Interstate, too? Good thing we're not out in it, right?" He paused for a moment and cleared his throat. "Well, it turns out I'm camped in Abigail's apartment. We brought some paperwork up here and..." He rolled his eyes. "I'm not surprised that you're not surprised."

He ducked his head and scuffed the carpet with his bare foot. "My truck's nearly buried. What's the routine around here? Does a snow plow come through?" He nodded. "Okay. I'll go out there first thing. Listen, don't let Dad shovel in the morning. I'll be over early. I'll either fix the snow blower or use the shovel. I—hi, Dad." He glanced at her and winked.

Well, good. Evidently he was fine with his parents knowing that he'd be spending the night with her and all that implied.

"Yes, sir, I know you're perfectly capable of shoveling, but you need to be fresh as a daisy to give your sermon, right? Promise you'll wait for me. Great. Love you both, too. I will. See you tomorrow." He disconnected. "My folks say hello."

"That's nice. And it's sweet that they called to check on you."

"Yeah, it is. My mom drives me crazy sometimes. And I love her with all my heart."

"I know you do." She stroked his lightly furred chest. "You have a really big heart, too, so that's a lot of love. You...what are you grinning about?"

"Delilah's sitting on my foot."

She glanced down. Sure enough, the dog's rump rested squarely on Luke's bare foot. Delilah looked up, her tongue lolling out in a doggie grin. "Does she do that for a reason?"

"To get my attention. She wants me to play with her."

"I'm fresh out of dog toys, but I—hang on, I have just the thing. I'll be right back." She started down the hall.

"I'll go with you." He followed her and so did his dog. "If you and I aren't headed back to your warm bed, I need my jeans and shirt."

"I could turn up the heat."

"That's silly."

"Not to me. I like the way you're dressed."

"Glad to hear it. But there's no point in jacking up the thermostat. After I play with Delilah for a while, she'll be ready to pack it in for the night. Me, too, in fact."

"You don't want to tackle more of the receipts?"

"Nope. In fact, how would you feel about spreading the job over several evenings?"

Yes. "You wouldn't want to drive home every night, I suppose."

"Wouldn't be practical. We might work late."

"Uh...I get up at three."

"So we wouldn't work late. But you never know when a storm might come up. Better to figure on staying."

She laughed. "Absolutely. You'd need to bring Delilah."

"I would."

"You might want to bring her food and her dishes."

"Definitely."

"And her bed."

"That, too."

"I've been thinking about how we'll handle her sleeping arrangement tonight." She opened her hall linen closet.

"Me, too, now that I know I won't be leaving. Which is awesome." He gave her a quick kiss on the cheek before walking into her bedroom.

She pulled a ragged towel from the bottom of the stack and raised her voice. "Since I don't have a dog bed, will an old quilt do?"

"I'm sure it will. Do you have one you could put down for her?"

"I do. I just need a stool to get it." With the towel in one hand, she went into the bedroom. "Once I bring it down, where should I put it?"

"At the end of the bed." He buttoned his jeans and zipped the fly before reaching for his shirt. "If you're okay with that."

Darned if he didn't look almost as sexy putting on his clothes as he had taking them off. "Whatever's the best solution, but I guess if she's in here with us, then you and I won't—"

"Oh, yes, we will. Unless you're tired of me already."

"But won't we disturb her?"

"Maybe not. We'll experiment. We can tone it down a bit. Closing the door was fine that first time because she was zonked and didn't even know we'd left. But if we shut her out all night after she's used to being in with me, she might think I was punishing her for something."

"I wouldn't want that."

He smiled. "You don't look too sure about it, though."

"Well, I—"

"I hope to spend more time in your bed, Abby. I'd like to have you spend time in mine. I want Delilah to get used to the idea."

Her body heated. "I see."

"Unless, like I said, you've already had enough of me."

She eliminated the space between them, cupped the back of his neck and pulled him down for a hot kiss involving lots of tongue. Then she backed away. "There's your answer."

He took a shaky breath. "Message received."

"And here's your dog toy."

"A towel?"

"Knot one end so she can bite into it and play tug-of-war with her."

"Cool! And you're sure you don't care what happens to this towel?"

"Sure don't. It's hers, now. While you two are playing, I'll make up her bed."

"Thank you. That would be great. Show me where the quilt is. I'll get it down for you."

"Linen closet, top shelf." She opened the door and pointed to the quilt.

"That looks like just what she needs." He reached up, lifted the quilt down and put it in her arms. "She'll be very happy with that. Thanks." He gave her a quick kiss. Then he patted his thigh. "Come on, pup. Let's go have some fun."

Delilah followed him down the hall.

"Hey, Luke, do you want dessert before we go to bed? I didn't offer you any tonight."

Laughing, he turned around and walked backward. "Yes, you did."

"I meant a bakery item, smart aleck. I have some double chocolate brownies in the refrigerator if that sounds good."

"With you, everything sounds good."

"Ditto, cowboy. Now go play with your doggie." She took the quilt into the bedroom. She'd designated it for picnics, although since moving here she hadn't gone on any. Or done much of anything recreational except recently, when Roxanne had suggested the occasional movie night in her apartment.

Roxanne and Ingrid would have noticed the heavy snow by now. Since she hadn't texted since cancelling on them earlier, they'd likely drawn their own conclusions. They wouldn't be surprised at the outcome, either.

Shaking out the quilt, she folded it into a size that resembled the dog bed at Luke's house. He was utterly devoted to that pup. With luck he'd get to keep her.

Delilah's playful growl drifted down the hall, followed by Luke's soft laughter. "Get it, pup! Come on, put your back into it!"

She gave the quilt a final pat, tightened the sash on her robe and walked down the hall. Her bare feet made no noise as she headed toward the playing field.

"Atta, girl! Look at that, you almost pulled me over! Go, Delilah, go!" More fierce growling and more laughter.

She paused at the end of the hall, entranced.

Luke had twirled the towel into a thick rope. He held one end with both hands and his dog gripped the knotted end with her strong teeth. Delilah back-peddled for all she was worth, stretching the towel tight.

He'd rolled back his sleeves and was making a great show of pulling hard. The muscles in his forearms bulged as if he could barely hold on. Yet considering his weight and strength, he could have dragged the dog around the room if he'd tried. Instead he only tugged enough to give her the thrill of competition. She clearly was having a great time. So was he, judging from his wide grin.

Abigail stood very still so they wouldn't notice her. As dog and man wrestled for possession of a raggedy towel, she quietly fell in love.

<u>20</u>

Luke was playing this by ear. He'd never had a dog, which meant he'd never dealt with the complication of keeping both his dog and his lady happy. He would have deferred to the lady's needs, but while he was busy doing that, his dog might think she'd done something wrong.

Consequently, he and Abigail had feasted on double chocolate brownies until Delilah had shown signs of winding down for the night. Then the little group headed back to the bedroom. It wasn't the most romantic setup, but it was the only one that made sense to him.

Delilah pranced down the hall, clearly thrilled to be going into the bedroom with them. He showed her the quilt. "This is your bed, pup."

She sniffed the quilt thoroughly before stepping on it with her front paws. Then she sniffed some more, put all four paws on it, circled and flopped down.

Abby let out a sigh of relief. "Thank goodness."

"I was hoping she'd react that way." He rubbed the back of his neck. "But now that she's settled, I'm not sure of the best way for us to—"

"Let's make it subtle." She walked around to the other side of the bed. "I'll take off my robe over here. You take off your clothes over there."

"At least I get to watch you do it."

"Same here." She untied her sash.

"You'll be finished before me."

"Uh-huh."

"Do me a favor. Take off your robe and just stand there. Let me look at you while I'm stripping down."

"All right." Drawing it off her shoulders, she let it fall to the floor.

Ahhh. Excellent idea. He smiled. "Nice."

She smiled back. "Thanks."

He looked his fill. Her short mop of curls gave her an air of innocence. She wasn't innocent, though. Her enthusiastic response earlier colored his view of her now.

As her nipples tightened, his fingers grew restless and moisture pooled in his mouth. His hands ached to cup her breasts, caress her hips, part her thighs and—

"One of us isn't taking off his clothes."

"Oh. Sorry." He wrenched at his shirt, popping snaps.

"Take your time."

He glanced across the expanse of mattress. Her eyes glowed with the same intensity burning in his gut. He slowed his movements.

As he peeled off his shirt, her gaze slid from his face to his chest and lingered there. He dropped the shirt and unfastened the button at his waist. She ran her tongue over her lips. He'd been aroused before, but now he was as hard as an axe handle.

Drawing down the zipper was painful, but he didn't rush it. Her breasts quivered as her breathing picked up. Shoving his jeans down, he kicked them away. She moaned softly.

At last he pulled off his boxers and stood before her, his cock fully erect. She took her time looking, too, and he didn't move. At last she lifted her head and gave him a slow, lazy grin. "That's done. Let's go to bed."

"Yes, ma'am." He climbed in and so did she. Shaking and on edge, he met her in the middle and pulled her close. "Now comes the challenge. Being quiet."

"Let me be on top."

"How will that help?"

"I don't know. I just want to. Roll over."

He was too tempted by the concept to argue. If she could be quiet riding him, he'd handle his reaction as best he could.

She straddled his thighs. "I have to get a condom out of the—"

"I will. My arms are longer." Reaching over, he opened the drawer and took out a holiday-wrapped packet. Last time he hadn't bothered to look at the tag. This time he did.

"What's it say?"

He grinned and swept a hand toward his bad boy standing at attention. "*Light a Candle.*"

"I do believe I will."

"Great view." He propped a pillow behind his head so he could more easily admire the quiver of her breasts as she unwrapped the condom and rolled it on.

"I'll bet you'll like the next part even better."

"I have a feeling I'm gonna love it."

"Maybe you should turn out the light, though. Like we're about to go to sleep."

"I've never felt more awake in my life." He pushed a small metal switch at the bottom and the cupcake lamp went out. Still not the time to ask her about it. Not when she was...holy moly, she was ready for action.

He swallowed a moan of delight as she eased down slowly, her palms braced on his chest. He clutched her hips. Not to guide her, not even to hurry the process along. Just to touch her silken skin as she took his happy cock deep into her warmth.

There. As close as two people could be. Magic. Even better than the first time.

She leaned down and brushed her lips over his. "I'm trying not to breathe too loud."

"Not easy." Sliding his hands upward, he cupped her breasts. "Can I do this?"

"Please do."

He squeezed gently. "You're sensitive here. Last time you whimpered."

She nibbled on his bottom lip. "I'm whimpering in my mind."

"I'm having a party in mine."

"Then let's bring on the entertainment." She lifted her hips, but not very far. Then she rotated them.

He sucked in air. "Oh, boy."

"Too much?"

"Didn't say that." He clenched his jaw to keep from coming. He blamed the unexpected move. He'd be ready next time. Coming in the first two minutes would not be cool.

"This motion should keep the bed from rocking as much." She did it again.

He managed to swallow his gasp. "Good call."

"You sound funny."

"Because my vocal cords want to yell and I won't let them."

"Yell in your mind." She swiveled her hips again.

"You wouldn't believe the noise I'm making in there."

"Me, too." She continued her erotic hip motion and her chest heaved. "This feels...really good."

"You're close?"

"Yeah. You?"

"I'm, um...not quite...." Then she added another twirl and he surrendered his pride. "Okay, I'm hanging on by a thread."

"Then let's both come. Quietly."

"Right." He let go of her beautiful breasts because he might pinch too hard and leave a mark. Instead he clenched his fists as she rotated first right, then left, then...his climax barreled through him. He was helpless to stop it, control it, or make sure she had one, too.

Then she impaled herself fully and the undulations flowing over his cock gave him the answer. She pressed her mouth against his shoulder for a moment before resting her cheek there.

Wrapping his arms around her quivering body, he silently offered thanks for whatever stars had aligned to give him this moment.

Her warm breath caressed his skin. "I think I bit you."

"Didn't feel it. Too busy enjoying myself."

"Normally I don't bite."

"But you were overcome with passion?"

She lifted her head. "As a matter of fact."

"Awesome." He could just barely make out her smile in the darkness. "I love that maneuver of yours, by the way. Creative. Sexy."

"And quiet."

"That, too."

"I don't think we disturbed her."

"Not so far. But I need to get up, so she might rouse herself then."

"Maybe not. She used up a lot of energy playing tug-of-war."

"So glad you suggested that." After Abby eased away, he climbed out of bed and went into her small bathroom to take care of the condom. The dark bar of soap in a dish by the sink filled the room with the scent of chocolate. Made him smile.

As did her willingness to let him call her Abby when she'd never encouraged anyone else to do it. Using a special name for her made their connection unique. The kind of relationship that might last a while.

Now there was a concept. He rinsed his hands and dried them on the towel hanging near the sink. Building a lasting relationship with a woman hadn't been on his radar. It was now.

People had a clever little catch-phrase for that concept. They called it falling in love. Was he? What they shared wasn't just about sex. Never had been.

The woman lying in the other room could become the most important person in his life. That idea took some getting used to. Didn't mean he didn't like it.

He walked back into the bedroom and peeked at Delilah to confirm that she was still out like a light. Climbing into the cozy bed, he reached for Abby and pulled her close.

She nestled against him with a sigh. "Are you okay?"

"Sure am." He stroked her back.

"You were gone so long I was afraid you'd fallen in." If she'd added the word *love* to that statement, she would've hit the nail on the head.

But she might not be ready to use that four-letter word, so he'd play it cool. "Just thinking about things."

"Like my messed-up records?"

"No, as a matter of fact." Twice she'd brought up the subject, so her anxiety about it wasn't gone. He searched for a change in topic. "Where did you find the cupcake lamp?"

"I didn't. My mom gave it to me when I graduated from culinary school. It was supposed to be a joke."

"But now it's not."

"Oh, it kind of is. I remember laughing with her about it. She said I didn't have to keep it. I'm glad I did."

"So am I." Oh, yeah, he was definitely falling.

"But I'm not fooled by that out-of-the-blue lamp question. You just didn't want to admit you were worrying about the records because you were afraid I'd start worrying."

"I swear to you I wasn't thinking about your paperwork. But now I am."

"Dammit. Screwed myself that time."

"Exactly." He chuckled. "Next time let me do it." The way he was heating up, that would be soon.

"Absolutely. I've learned my lesson." She reached down and wrapped her fingers around his thickening cock. "But I'll bet I can convince you to forget about my paperwork."

"Guaranteed." He grasped her wrist. "Except I need to ask something before you proceed. Is it okay if I bring over some clothes and stuff tomorrow. It would save time if I don't have to drive back home every morning to get cleaned up."

"I have to get up at three. You might hate that."

He let go of her wrist. "If I do, that's my problem." Might as well find out before he was in too deep. Ha. Like it wasn't already too late.

21

The rumbling of the Eagles Nest snowplow woke Abigail before dawn. Evidently making love most of the night had worn her out enough that she'd slept in later than normal for a Sunday. She was alone in the bed but Luke was still in the apartment. Light and his soft conversation with Delilah came from the direction of the living room.

Quickly slipping into her robe, she walked down the hallway. Luke was putting on his jacket and Delilah danced around him, tail wagging.

"I was about to come in and tell you goodbye." He walked over and drew her close. The dog followed and continued her cavorting. He glanced down. "Delilah, sit." Her haunches dropped but she quivered with excitement.

Abigail smiled. "She's racing around in her mind."

"Yeah, she is. Crazy dog. Anyway, I'm going down to see if the snow removal guys will help me get my truck out."

"Is that even possible? Last night it looked buried."

"It's not so bad, now. We must have had another pretty good wind come up. It rearranged the snow a bit."

"Want me to keep Delilah here while you go check?"

"I would, but she needs to go out, so I might as well take her with me now."

"What if the snow's piled up against the door?"

"Then I'll tunnel through. I'm hoping it's not completely blocked, though. Can't see too well from up here. Only thing is, once I'm out, I'll need you to lock up after me."

"I'll get my slippers."

"And your coat. Don't want you to freeze while Delilah and I are navigating the door situation."

"Be right back." Walking in the bedroom, she glanced longingly at the rumpled sheets. No lazy Sunday morning with Luke.

But he'd promised his dad he'd come over. Mustn't be greedy. She pulled on her sheepskin slippers and grabbed her coat.

He stood waiting, Delilah's leash already clipped to her collar. "I wish I didn't have to leave."

"I wish you didn't, either, but we had a lot of snow and I'm sure your dad could use some help."

"Do you have to go anywhere today? I could come back and dig out your vehicle."

She shook her head. "That's very sweet, but since I doubt we'll go horseback riding—"

"I forgot about that. I'm guessing the ranch is socked in. It'll be sundown before all the roads are clear. I might need to ask Zane if he'd plow mine."

She zipped up her coat. "Let's take it one thing at a time. First job is to get you and Delilah out the front door."

"Wrong." He slipped a hand around her waist and pulled her in tight. "First job is to kiss you. With great care. My beard is wicked in the morning."

"Makes you look a little bit wicked, too. Sexy."

"From a distance, maybe. I could sand the floor of my house with my chin right now. Just hold still."

"I don't care if you...mm." The touch of his mouth stirred her up like it had last night. Even better, his tongue tasted of chocolate.

Way too soon, he drew back, regret in his gaze. "Like I said, wish I could stay."

"Then you could have more of those brownies you just snitched."

"Then I could have more of everything." He heaved a sigh. "But I gotta go. I hope the lock isn't frozen shut."

"Maybe I should go get my hair dryer."

"There's an outlet down there?"

"No, but I have the world's longest extension cord."

"I'll think positive. I'll be able to break free so Delilah and I can brave the drifts. Let's go."

Abigail followed them down the stairs. "She likes the cold weather, though, right?"

"She's a natural in the snow. I'm convinced she was born and bred here."

"Then this is where she belongs." The stairwell grew more frigid with each step down.

"That decision might not be ours to make." He reached the bottom. "If you'll hold the leash, I'll see what the story is with the door." He handed it over and put on his gloves and hat.

The lock was stubborn but finally surrendered to his strong grip. "Now to see if it'll open or not."

Abigail stomped her feet to keep warm. But standing there wasn't such a hardship. She had a ringside seat as Luke displayed his manly strength.

With his morning scruff, he looked bold and slightly dangerous, as if he might sweep her up in his arms and carry her off...somewhere. And then ravish her.

Swearing softly, he tugged on the knob. Then he braced his feet and pulled hard. The door gave way with a loud crunch and he staggered back just as Roxanne appeared in her pajamas, her dark hair in disarray.

"Is everything okay down there?"

"It's fine," Luke said. "Sorry if I woke you."

"I hear talking." Ingrid came out, also in her pajamas, a sleep mask pushed up to her forehead. "What's going on?"

"Just trying to get out," Luke said. "I didn't think about how much noise I was making in the process."

"It's okay," Roxanne said. "Just so you've been treating Abigail right."

He reddened. "Well, ma'am, I—"

"He has." Abigail smiled at Roxanne.

"Woo-hoo! That's what we want to hear, right, Ingrid?"

"Right you are, Rox. Well done, Luke!"

"He had to get out the door because he promised to shovel snow at his parents' house," Abigail said.

A chorus of *aww, how sweet* came from the top of the stairs, which made him blush even more.

She gave him a quick kiss on his bristly cheek. "See you later, cowboy."

"You bet." He climbed over the knee-high drift and Delilah took the hurdle with joyful abandon. Then they made tracks for the plow and the truck that followed it. One member of the crew was already working on Luke's truck with an industrial-strength snow blower.

"They'll dig him out," Roxanne said.

"Looks like it." Abigail locked the door and climbed the stairs.

"Hey, are you both coming to my place for coffee and two-day-old pastries?"

"Sure." Ingrid started toward Roxanne's apartment. "Once I'm awake, I'm awake."

Roxanne put her arm around Abigail's shoulders. "Your evening went well, then?"

"Very well."

"Good." Roxanne gave a quick squeeze. "Glad to know the packaging delivered on the promise."

* * *

Luke made it to his folks' house before his dad had started shoveling, although lights were on inside. The plow had come along and the street was clear so Luke parked there. He let Delilah out to frolic in the huge drifts the plow had created.

The plow had taken care of the street but blocked the driveways. He was looking at several hours of work if he couldn't fix the blower.

Hey, look at that. Here came Badger in his big red truck. Great timing.

Badger pulled in behind Luke and climbed out. "Fancy meetin' you here." His breath fogged the air.

"Didn't want my dad shoveling when he has a sermon to give."

"Had the same thought. Hey, pup!" He crouched down to scratch behind Delilah's ears. "Somebody's been rollin' in the snow."

"Yeah, I'll have to towel her off before I let her in the house."

Badger stood. "Kinda surprised to see you here, though. How'd you get your truck down that windin' road of yours?"

"I didn't stay there last night."

"Where'd you...oh, I get it." He glanced at the house. "Do your folks know?"

"Yep. Mom called last night after the blizzard hit to make sure I was okay. I said I was at Abby's. I mean, Abigail's."

Badger's eyebrows lifted. "Abby, is it?"

"She says I can call her that."

"You should see your face. You're a goner, buddy."

"That's a possibility."

"You do realize this new situation of yours could throw your momma into weddin' mode."

"I know, but I—"

"Five bucks says she'll mention a double weddin' before we leave the house."

"I'll take that bet. She's reformed."

"Uh-uh. She's in stealth mode."

"We'll find out. I want to grab a cup of coffee before we start."

"Me, too. Ten bucks says she'll bring it up before we finish our coffee."

"You're on."

"By the way, do your folks own a snow-blower?"

"Listen to you talking like a Montana boy! I'm surprised you know such a thing exists, you being from Atlanta."

"I catch on quick."

"They have a blower, but it's on the fritz. I thought I'd try to fix it before we haul out the shovels."

"I reckon I can fix it."

"You? The guy who can't hammer a nail straight to save his soul?"

"We're not talkin' about carpentry. We're talkin' about engines. That's where I shine."

"That's excellent news. Let's do this thing. It's damn cold out here."

"After you." Badger gestured toward the house.

"Is that so I can forge a path for your Southern ass?"

Badger laughed. "Told you I catch on quick."

The porch had been somewhat protected and the snow wasn't very deep there. Luke brushed off his Wranglers. That's what he got for clearing a path. Badger's jeans were almost snow-free.

Luke tapped on the front door. Soon his dad opened it dressed in corduroy pants at least twenty years old and a flannel shirt of the same vintage.

"I heard you boys drive up. Come on in before crucial body parts freeze and fall off."

"We're okay," Luke said. "But we need—"

"I'm talking about my body parts." His dad grinned. "You're young. Yours are fine."

"First we need some towels laid down in the entry and one I can use for Delilah."

"Ah. Gotcha." He closed the door.

"I want a pair of those corduroy pants," Badger said. "I'll bet they're warm as toast."

"I'm sure they are but you'll look like a dork."

"At least I'd be a warm dork. Your dad doesn't care how he looks. That's awesome."

"What's awesome?" Luke's dad opened the door and handed out a couple of towels.

"Your pants," Badger said.

"I *know*." He stuck his hands in the pockets and rocked back on his heels. "Bought these five years after Virginia and I got married. Every so often she tries to give them to Goodwill, so now I check the bag before it goes out the door."

"Think I could find a pair like that at the Goodwill?"

"Worth a try." He gestured toward the towels. "Use those for Delilah. I've spread a couple more in the entry. Luke, your mother wants to know if Delilah's had breakfast."

"Not yet. So if you wouldn't mind giving her some of the kibble you bought—"

"Of course not. Want me to pour you both some coffee?"

"Please," Luke said. "Thanks, Dad."

The door closed again and Luke used the towels on his dog. He got Badger to pick her up so he could wipe her paws before they went in.

Once they were through the door, Badger sighed with pleasure. "I'm gettin' better about the cold, but warm is still my happy place."

"I hear my granddog out there!" Luke's mom came out of the kitchen wearing a dark blue sweat suit. Delilah trotted over to sit right in front of her with a big doggie grin.

"Who's a good girl?" His mom reached into her pocket.

Delilah whined and thumped her tail.

"I know! You are!" She gave the dog a biscuit before smiling at Luke and Badger. "Such good boys. Thank you both for coming."

Luke hung his jacket and hat on the coat tree. "Badger says he can fix the blower."

"That would be fabulous. Come on, Delilah. Grandma's got your breakfast ready. Coffee's poured, boys."

"Thanks, ma'am." Badger hung his coat and hat next to Luke's and lowered his voice. "Want to make it twenty?"

"Sure."

They gathered around the kitchen table and Luke's mom brought over a plate of mini cinnamon rolls. "From Pie in the Sky," she said with a wink in Luke's direction. "I'll make you a real breakfast when you're done outside, but this will give you something in your stomach."

"Appreciate it, Mom." Luke reached for a roll and bit into it. Mm. Abby did good work. He finished it off and picked up another.

"These are delicious." His dad took seconds, too. "Abigail has skills."

"I totally agree." Badger was scarfing them down.

Luke's mother wasn't eating rolls or drinking her coffee. That was a bad sign that something was on her mind.

Luke gestured to the plate. "Bet you can't eat just one."

"I'll have one in a minute."

Uh-oh.

"I've been thinking that since Hayley's coming in next weekend, we should have a family dinner either Saturday or Sunday night. Do either of you boys have a preference?"

"Whatever works for Hayley." Badger picked up another cinnamon roll.

"I could do either," Luke said.

"Would you like to bring Abigail?"

"Um, I can certainly ask her." He avoided looking at Badger.

"If she can make it, then she and Hayley could get to know each other better."

Luke nodded. "True."

"I hope she can come." His mother beamed at him. "As Badger would say, those two will get along like grits and gravy."

"They probably will." Luke's coffee had cooled and he could drink instead of sip. He took bigger gulps. Time to leave the kitchen before—

"Look, I'm not going to push anybody into anything."

"Virginia..." Luke's dad glanced at her.

"Don't worry, Warren. I'm not scheming, I promise. But since I have Luke and Badger here, it makes sense to at least plant the seed of an idea."

"You know what, Mom? It's way too early in the morning to be planting seeds of ideas in my head. I'll just forget it. But thanks for the coffee." He stood. "If you'll excuse us, we should start working on that blower. Badger, you about ready?"

"Just a few more sips." He hid a smile behind his raised cup.

"Then I'll make it quick," his mother said. "Two words. Double wedding."

22

By mid-week, coffee sales hadn't slacked off as Abigail had feared. They'd dropped a little from the initial launch but were steady. Doug had the day off and Yolanda was on break, leaving Abigail and Ingrid holding down the fort.

The shop was still empty of patrons when Ingrid called over from the coffee machine. "Since no one's here right now, I'm treating myself to a latte. Want one?"

"Sure. Want a chocolate chip cookie?"

"Absolutely."

"Coming up." She put two cookies on a plate, grabbed a couple of napkins and walked over to a bistro table.

"I kind of like having the place to ourselves." Ingrid set down their lattes and pulled out a chair.

"Me, too." She sipped her latte. "You make a damned good coffee drink, girlfriend."

"Thanks. You make a damned good cookie."

She laughed. "Thanks. We're amazing."

"Yep. So tell me, how's it going with Luke?"

"It's...nice." Her cheeks heated.

"Just nice?"

"No. It's wonderful."

"*That's* what I wanted to see. You just lit up right then."

"I'm not surprised. He's so...kind. I've shown him my screwed up record keeping, and he's not judging me."

"What a relief that must be."

"You have no idea. I'm still a little embarrassed that I let things get so bad, but one smile from Luke and I get over it."

"Wow. You're serious about the guy."

"I am. And I could be wrong, but I think he's serious about me."

Ingrid studied her. "You're not wrong. I've seen how he looks at you. But I am curious as to how you see it working out logistically once your files are in order. You'd think he'd want to spend time at his house."

"I'm sure he does. He backed off on the renovations because he's not out there very often to help."

"Would you consider moving out there?"

"It wouldn't be as convenient. Besides, he hasn't asked me."

"You might have to get creative. Spend some time out there and some time in your apartment."

She nodded. "Where did Roxanne take off to this morning?"

"She drove into Bozeman to pick up some electronic thingamajig that will boost some other doohickey related to her current job. I don't pretend to understand, but she was excited."

"She does get excited about her work. I predict that she—"

The front door opened and Kendra came in.

Abigail stood and brushed cookie crumbs from her fingers so she could go over and give her a hug. "It's so good to see you!"

"I want a hug, too." Ingrid left her chair. "Have you been in since last week? I don't remember seeing you."

"I haven't been in." Kendra embraced her. "I meant to, and then we had that huge snow Saturday night. Took some time to dig out of that. Luckily I have a lot of helpers."

"Luke mentioned that he's been out a couple of times when he didn't have client appointments," Abigail said.

"He has." She smiled. "He's a good guy."

"Sure is."

"What can we get for you?" Ingrid gestured toward the coffee machine. "I've come up with a Valentine coffee I call *Love at First Sight.*"

Kendra laughed. "What's in it?"

"Chocolate and amaretto, topped with a dollop of whipped cream and a candy message heart. I shake the package and dump one out. I let Fate choose what the message will be."

"After that buildup, how can I resist?"

"That's the idea. One *Love at First Sight* coming up."

"Anything from the bakery case?" Abigail wandered over to it and Kendra followed her.

"Please. I'm out of brownies and lately I've been craving cherry pie."

"I only have one left. They're popular this time of year."

"Is it a Valentine's Day thing?"

"Nope." Abigail grinned. "George Washington's birthday."

"You're pulling my leg."

"It's the truth. After Valentine's Day is over, customers still buy cherry pies. Where I worked in Rapid City, we always had a run on them in February."

"No kidding?"

"It's logical." Behind her, the front door opened. Ingrid welcomed the customer, so Abigail finished her explanation. "George Washington leads to cherry tree which leads to cherry pie. Bingo, you crave cherry pie in February, all because of good old George."

"Huh."

"Sounds right to me," said the customer who'd just come in. "I've been wanting cherry pie lately, too."

Abigail turned. If the man was from Eagles Nest, she'd never seen him before.

He was tall, maybe six-five, with the wide shoulders and muscular chest of someone who was used to physical work. His legs were slightly bowed, like many of the cowboys around here, including all the McGavin brothers.

He took off his Stetson to reveal thick brown hair shot through with silver. "I'm Quinn Sawyer, Roxanne's dad. Is she around?"

"Oh, my gosh, no, she's not." She took his hand in both of hers and squeezed. "I'm Abigail. It's so good to meet you. Roxanne went to Bozeman this morning. When's she due back, Ingrid?"

"She'll show up any time now. I'll text her." She hurried over with Kendra's drink. "Here's your *Love at First Sight.*"

Roxanne's dad smiled at Kendra. "Your what?"

She held it up. "It's a Valentine drink."

"I could make you one, Mr. Sawyer."

"Quinn."

"Quinn. I'm Ingrid, by the way."

"I figured. Pleased to meet you, ma'am." He shook her hand. "Roxanne thinks a lot of you ladies."

"We think a lot of her, too. Can I make you one of those drinks? It'll be on the house." She looked at Abigail, eyebrows raised.

"Of course." No way was she charging Roxanne's dad for a coffee drink.

"I don't know if I should have one." He glanced at Kendra. "Have you tried yours?"

"Not yet. Want me to?"

"Please, if you would, ma'am. Then I can find out whether it makes you fall in love on the spot."

She grinned. "It's coffee, not a love potion."

"You can't be too careful with this sort of thing. I notice it's topped with one of those little candy hearts with something written on it, maybe a magic spell. What's it say?"

"Let me check." She turned the drink so she could read it. "*I'm yours.*"

"Now, see, those are two powerful words. No telling what's going to happen when you take a drink."

"We're about to find out." She tipped the cup and took a slow swallow. Lowering the cup, she stared at him as if in a trance. "Quinn."

"Yes, ma'am?" His mouth twitched and his eyes sparkled.

Kendra spoke slowly, like a woman possessed. "Take. Me. Darling. I. Am. Yours."

His deep laughter spilled out. Abigail and Ingrid exchanged a grin, but Kendra maintained a straight face for several seconds. Then she started laughing so hard she had to put her drink down or risk dumping it.

Quinn seemed to enjoy the joke the most, though. Pulling a bandana out of his back pocket, he wiped his streaming eyes. Just when he seemed to have recovered himself, he'd look at Kendra and start laughing again.

Eventually he caught his breath. "Thank you, ma'am."

"Kendra." She held out her hand. "Kendra McGavin. I own Wild Creek Ranch."

"It's a pleasure, Kendra. I can't remember the last time I've—"

"Dad!" Roxanne burst through the front door and threw herself into his arms. "Why didn't you say you were coming?"

He hugged her tight. "Wanted to surprise you, honeybun. Thought you were around most of the time."

"Usually I am. Wouldn't you know I'd decide to go to Bozeman today. How long have you been here?"

"Long enough to meet your friends and Kendra."

"Well, there you go. That's an impressive list for someone who just blew into town. I saw your truck parked outside and couldn't believe it. How long can you stay?"

"A few hours. Then I'll head back."

"Sure is a lot of driving, Dad. You can have my bed and I'll sleep on the couch tonight."

He shook his head. "Appreciate the offer, honeybun, but that's exactly what I don't want, to put you out. I just figured since I've never been here, I ought to see the place. I like it so far."

"You might want to take him to the GG for lunch," Kendra said. "Best burgers in town."

He turned to her. "What's the GG?"

"The Guzzling Grizzly. My son co-owns it."

He blinked. "Stepson?"

"No, my biological son."

"Sorry, ma'am, but you don't look old enough to—"

"I had him when I was very young. All of them, in fact."

"Kendra has five boys, Dad, all grown."

His gaze swung back to her. "I'll be damned." He cleared his throat. "Excuse my language, but I figured you for around thirty-five."

"Keep that up and I might fall in love with you for real. I'm forty-five."

"You don't look it."

"Thank you." She glanced at Roxanne. "If your dad's on a tight schedule, you'd better skedaddle so you can beat the noon rush."

"Good advice. Come on, Dad. Let's grab lunch."

"Sounds good." He looked at Abigail. "I'll stop here before I leave so I can say a proper goodbye. And if you'd put aside a cherry pie for me, I'd be much obliged."

"Well, I—"

"It'll knock your socks off." Kendra looked at Abigail and gave her a little head shake. "You'll want to make the drive again next week just to get another one."

"I just might, at that." He settled his hat on his head. "Abigail and Ingrid, I'll see you later. Kendra, it was nice meeting you."

"Same here, Quinn." She waited until they were out the door. "Where does he live?"

"Near Spokane, I think," Abigail said. "Does that sound right, Ingrid?"

"That's what I remember Rox saying. He has a ranch there."

Kendra sighed. "Yeah, well, that's probably for the best. Besides, he didn't come in on a motorcycle and he doesn't have a mustache."

"A motorcycle and a mustache?" Abigail frowned at Ingrid. "Is this making sense to you?"

"Nope."

"Here's the scoop," Kendra said. "Trevor and I were talking one night and he came up with this image of a guy he thought would be perfect for me."

"Have you ever dated?" Abigail cringed. "Sorry, that might be too personal."

"It's not too personal, and no, I haven't. Ian died when the boys were little and I just...never considered it. But evidently my boys are worried that I'll be lonely now that they're all out of the house. I'm not lonely, but it's hard to convince them."

Ingrid leaned against the counter. "That doesn't explain the motorcycle and the mustache."

"Sounds like a short that comes before the main feature." Kendra smiled. "The motorcycle was Trevor's idea. He said my perfect guy would ride into town on one, but he'd still be a cowboy. These days he wouldn't come galloping into town on his horse unless he's some nut job."

Abigail laughed. "Just what you don't want, some yahoo who thinks he's a rhinestone cowboy. A motorcycle works, though. And he had a mustache?"

"Right." She glanced at Ingrid. "What are you doing?"

"Texting Rox." She studied her screen. "Ha! Her dad has a motorcycle."

"Oh, my gosh!" Abigail pressed her hand to her chest. "That's freaky."

"But no mustache," Kendra said.

Ingrid tucked her phone away. "No problem. He could grow one."

"Yes, but he would still live in Washington." She drained her coffee. "That was delicious. Let me take my brownies and go home."

Abigail boxed the brownies and rang up the sale before giving Kendra a hug goodbye.

Ingrid came over to hug her, too. Ever since the launch of the specialty coffee, Kendra and the other Whine and Cheese ladies were VIP customers at Pie in the Sky.

"She really liked him," Ingrid said as Kendra climbed in the ranch van. "She gave up her cherry pie for him."

"He really liked her, too. Did you see how he kept laughing? He was intrigued. Very intrigued."

"But he lives in Washington."

Abigail looked at her. "Your boyfriend lives in Boston."

"And I'm here to tell you it's no fun. The best is to be in the same town. No, that's not right. The best is to be under the same roof."

"I know." Being under the same roof with Luke had been incredible. But she had no idea how they'd manage that feat going forward.

23

Luke disconnected the call and his chest tightened when he looked at Delilah. This really, really, sucked.

He cleared his throat. "Somebody brought another flyer to the shelter, pup. This time the number's clearly visible."

She picked up on his tone immediately. Instead of smiling and wagging her tail, she came over, laid her head on his knee and gazed up at him with a worried expression. Like she could read his mind.

"I have to call." He ruffled her ears. "Maybe they had a legitimate reason for not following up. I need to give them a chance to explain. And if the reason's good enough..." He chose not to finish the sentence.

And today had been such a good one, too. He'd met with a new client this morning and he'd spent the afternoon in his office pulling together a marketing plan for his mom's barn venue.

In about fifteen minutes he'd leave for Pie in the Sky. He'd estimated that he and Abby would need a week to sort and record everything in the box, but it was only Wednesday and they were almost done.

He might have to slow down. He loved the dynamic and wasn't eager to change it. The routine allowed them to get to know each other, in bed and out.

Everything had been going great. Now this. He set his phone down because holding it was a reminder of what he had to do. Abby wouldn't like this any better than he did. She'd been so convinced no one would claim Delilah. Or whatever the dog's real name was.

"You know what, pup? Let's make the call from Abby's apartment. That way I can put the phone on speaker and she can hear what the person has to say. I'll feel better if she's there to help me evaluate whether they should get you back. Because they won't if they're the least bit dicey."

She wagged her tail in slow motion, as if she understood something critical was on the line.

"Okay. We have a game plan." Likely the people weren't dicey. As Kendra had said, Delilah wouldn't be such a good dog if she'd come from a bad home. But he'd cling to the possibility, anyway, because he couldn't imagine this house without Delilah in it.

He arrived at the bakery as Abby and Ingrid were tidying up in preparation for closing. He unsnapped the leash so they could each give his dog a biscuit. No, not *his* dog. Calling her that was a bad habit that had crept up on him.

Both women fussed over Delilah. It was hard to watch when it could be the end of such rituals.

Abby glanced at him. "Are you all right?"

"Sure." He snapped out of his funk.

"Is there a problem with a client?"

"No, ma'am." He smiled. "Maybe I just need a biscuit."

"Why didn't you say so?" She pulled an oatmeal raisin cookie out of the case and brought it to him. "Do you know any tricks?"

"Tons. Remind me and I'll show you some later."

"Okay, you two lovebirds," Ingrid called over. "Have pity on the lonely and frustrated among you."

"Sorry, Ingrid," he called back. "When's that guy of yours coming out?"

"Spring."

Spring. He'd looked forward to warm weather and long rides through meadows of wildflowers. Wouldn't be as much fun, now. Spot On would miss Delilah, too. They'd become buddies.

"You're doing it again."

"What?"

"The sad eyes."

"You'd be sad, too, if someone promised you a cookie and didn't deliver."

"Here's your cookie," she said gently.

"Thanks." He lowered his voice. "I'll tell you when we get upstairs."

"Okay." She blew him a kiss and went back to cleaning out the bakery case.

"Is the trash ready to go out?"

"Sure is."

"All righty, Delilah! Get the trash, girl!"

She pranced over and picked up one bulging bag gently in her teeth. He grabbed the other. Clipping the leash to her collar, he led her out the door and around to the bin in the alley.

She'd learned the trick in about thirty minutes of practice on Monday afternoon. Remarkable dog. If the people who'd put out the flyer didn't understand how special she was, then they weren't getting her. But they probably did know.

By the time he came back, Ingrid was on her way out the door and Abby was right behind her.

She locked up quickly. "That does it for today." She stroked Delilah's head. "Thanks for taking out the trash, you two. Great teamwork."

"Yes, ma'am."

Ingrid held the outside door for them and they all trooped upstairs.

"I'll be in Roxanne's room if you need me for anything," Ingrid said over her shoulder.

"Are you going to tell her about the cherry pie?"

"Sure, why not? She'll get a kick out of knowing her dad was such a hit."

"Her dad was here?" News to him.

"Just for a few hours," Abby said. "Drove from Spokane."

"Hefty drive to do twice in one day."

"He seemed fine with it." She unzipped her parka as she topped the stairs and walked the short distance to her place.

Normally he couldn't wait to be alone with her. But today he had bad news or what could be bad news. For them, at least. Maybe not for Delilah.

She turned as he closed the door behind him and unclipped Delilah's leash. "What is it?"

"I have the number for the people who put out the flyer."

"Oh, Luke." Her shoulders sagged. "I take it you haven't called."

"I decided to wait so you could hear the call and help me judge whether they measure up."

"Good. I'm glad you did. And maybe she's not the dog in the flyer."

"She is. You know she is."

Delilah had gone to her toy box and picked up the leg she'd chewed off one of her stuffed animals. Ever since she'd amputated that leg, she'd enjoyed strolling around with it dangling out of her mouth.

Normally it made him laugh. Not today.

"Ask them to describe her in detail." Abby took off her parka and went to the hall closet. "Not just what she looks like, but how she acts." She hung up her parka and stepped back.

He put his jacket on a hanger and laid his hat on a shelf she'd cleared for him. "Like the way she waits for one of us to tell her it's okay to eat. They should mention that. It's distinctive." He went back to the living room, pulled out his phone and started pacing. "What else?"

"They should tell you she's brilliant, the smartest dog they've ever had."

He nodded. "What about her affinity for horses and ranch life? Kendra thinks she lived on one."

"Maybe, but that might be instinct kicking in. But the herding thing she does with her peeps—they should definitely tell you about that."

"Yeah."

"Thank you for letting me be a part of this."

He held her gaze. "I could pretend I did it for your sake, but really it's for mine. I wanted you with me."

Her eyes glowed with emotion. "That's...good to hear."

He took a shaky breath and scrolled through his contacts for the one marked *Delilah*. "Okay. Calling, now." He tapped the number and put the call on speaker.

"Hello?" The woman who answered sounded elderly.

"Ma'am, my name's Luke Bennett and I'm calling from Montana." His heart raced. "I have a dog here who might be the one you lost."

"You mean Daisy? You found Daisy?"

"Maybe. If you could describe your dog, ma'am, we'll see if it's the same—"

"Let me get my husband. He spent more time with her than I did."

Luke glanced at Abby.

She was frowning. "Suspicious," she murmured. "If she's lived with a dog, she should be able to—"

"Hello?" The guy sounded elderly, too. "Mr. Bennett, is it?"

"Yes, sir. I think I might have—"

"Right, right. Daisy. Jumped out of the car at a rest stop. We didn't have a crate for her, see, and I had to get out to use the restroom. She bolted and disappeared. Snowing, you know."

"I do know."

"We went back to Bozeman, had some flyers printed, waited for the snow to let up and posted them around town. Didn't think it would do much good."

His description of the circumstances gnawed at Luke's remaining kernel of hope. "I got your number from a flyer."

"Huh. Amazing."

"Sir, if you could describe your dog, that will help us decide—"

"All black except for this white patch on her chest. Floppy ears. Think she has quite a bit of border collie in her."

Luke bowed his head. "I see. Could you...ah...describe her behavior, anything unusual she does?"

"Let me think. Oh, one peculiar thing about Daisy. My brother was a devout man and he taught that dog to wait while he said grace over her food. She won't eat until you tell her to go ahead. She's waiting for the prayer to end."

It was her. Luke glanced at Abby. Her eyes glimmered with tears and she'd pressed her hand to her mouth. He looked away again. Somehow he had to get through this conversation.

"She was your brother's dog?"

"Yes, sir."

"How long have you had her?"

"Oh, I guess we had her about a week."

"A *week*?"

"That's how long it took us to handle the funeral arrangements, sort out the legalities of the trust and hire a real estate agent to sell the ranch. My brother had things well organized, though. We packed up the few family items we wanted, took the dog, and headed back here."

"I suppose she's special to you, since she was your brother's dog. You probably—"

"Actually, my wife's not a dog person, but we felt obligated. When your brother dies, and entrusts his beloved dog to you, you can't just drop her off at a shelter. Some might, but we couldn't."

Hope became a warm place in Luke's heart. "Are you saying you're not eager to have her back?"

"I'm saying that we'll come get her because we don't expect others like yourself to assume our burdens."

"Sir, she's not a burden to me." The warm place expanded. He risked looking at Abby. Tears ran down her cheeks but her expression was pure joy. "In fact, with your permission, I'd be honored to keep her."

"You're a dog person?"

"Evidently so. Or at least I'm this dog's person."

Abby sniffed. Then she knelt, wrapped her arms around Delilah and buried her face in the dog's thick ruff. Delilah gazed at him and smiled.

"Do you have room for her to run around? She needs that. We retired to a patio home with a postage stamp for a yard. I hadn't figured out how I'd—"

"I have all kinds of room." Adrenaline made his voice shake and he paused to take a breath. "Five acres. I live next door to a big ranch. That's where I stable my horse."

"Son, that's exactly what Daisy needs, way better than bringing her down here to live with us. By the way, how'd you happen to find her?"

Luke swallowed. "I didn't. She found me."

24

Abigail kept her tear-streaked face tucked into Delilah's thick coat while she waited for Luke to wind up the conversation. Now that Delilah's caretaker had been relieved of another wintertime drive to Montana, he became chatty.

Typical of Luke, he was kind and accommodating. He promised to send pictures of Delilah/Daisy in her new surroundings. The couple didn't have a computer or smart phones, so he asked for their mailing address. He also got the name of Delilah's vet so he could find out whether she was current on her shots.

After several minutes of chit-chat punctuated with Luke's soft chuckle, he bid the old fellow goodbye and disconnected.

Lifting her head, Abigail looked at him. "Want to join us? We're trying to have a group hug, but I don't think you can call it a group with two."

"No, you need at least three." He dropped to his knees on Delilah's other side. Then he wrapped his arms around the dog and Abigail. "This qualifies as a group hug." He gazed into her eyes. "She's ours, Abby."

Tears threatened again. "Mostly yours. You found her, and you—"

"You loaned me a scarf to make a leash. You let her come into the bakery. You welcomed her up here."

"I know, but—"

"You kept insisting she'd end up being my dog when I was afraid to believe it. I'm the one who got her off the highway, but you've been her champion from the start. There's a reason I couldn't make that call without you."

She treasured every word of praise from this loving man. "I wouldn't have missed it for the world."

"It could have gone the other way."

"I wouldn't have missed it for the world, whichever way it turned out."

His breath hitched. "That's a powerful lot of support, lady."

"No more than you're willing to give me."

"I'm glad you know that." He leaned closer, slightly squashing the dog between them. "This calls for a kiss."

She inched closer, too. Delilah didn't seem to mind. "Am I kissing you or are you kissing me?"

"We're kissing each other."

"That works." She met him in the middle. A very happy, very warm dog separated them, but Luke's mouth on hers still gave her a buzz.

Evidently he had the same reaction because he strained to get closer yet. Delilah protested with a whine. Wriggling free, she sent them sprawling.

Abigail got the giggles. Pushing herself to a sitting position, she glanced at Luke, who'd propped himself on his elbows. His happy grin gladdened her heart.

He glanced at Delilah, who'd retrieved the amputated leg of her toy before going on walkabout. "I almost can't believe it turned out this way."

Abigail nudged him with her foot. "But it did."

"My dad is going to love the part about praying over the dog food. I can't wait to tell him."

As if on cue, Delilah came out of the kitchen with her food bowl in her mouth.

Abigail laughed. "Has she ever done that before?"

"No, ma'am." Luke got to his feet and offered Abigail a hand up. "But I think it means she's settling in."

"Are you going to change her name back to what it was?"

"What do you think about it?" He walked into the kitchen and the dog followed with her empty dish.

"I'm used to Delilah so I may be prejudiced. But it seems to suit the dog I know better than Daisy. It's edgier. More complicated. Don't laugh, but I think she has a rich inner life."

He smiled.

"See, you're laughing."

"Nope. I'm smiling because I agree with you. Stuff's going on in that brain of hers all the time." He took the bowl from Delilah. "Isn't it pup? Always thinking, aren't you?"

She wagged her tail and gave him her doggie grin.

"Got me figured out, too." He put food in her bowl and set it on the floor, where it sat untouched as Delilah waited for permission to eat.

He hesitated. "Um, Abby, would you think it was too weird if we—"

"Offered a blessing? I think it's appropriate after what just happened." She held out her hand to him. "I'll leave the wording up to you. You're the preacher's son."

"I see. Pressure's on." But he squeezed her hand and began speaking in a soft, reverent tone.

She closed her eyes to better enjoy the velvet sound of his voice.

After giving thanks in global terms, he moved on to specifics, mentioning family members by name. But when he said he was grateful for her, she nearly fell over. He named Delilah next, murmured a gentle *amen* and the blessing was complete, although he didn't release her hand.

When she opened her eyes, the dog remained sitting in front of her bowl the way she always had, but she appeared more...settled. "I think she liked that."

"I think so, too." Reaching down, he scratched the top of Delilah's head with his free hand. "Okay, girl. You can eat."

She began munching away.

"Maybe we should grab some dinner, too," Abigail said. "There's leftover—"

"Can I have a raincheck?"

"On dinner?"

"I have something more important in mind." Tugging gently, he pulled her out of the kitchen. "We need to celebrate." He led her through the living room and down the hall. "With the door closed."

"What about Delilah?"

"She has food, a cozy place and her toys. I'll bet she even knows that she's with us for good. She'll be fine."

With us for good. Dazzled by the implied commitment, she went into his arms the moment he closed the door. Cupping his face in both hands, she gazed into his warm brown eyes. "You mentioned me in the blessing. I didn't expect that."

"No?" He smiled. "Then maybe I haven't been showing my gratitude properly." He began to undress her, kissing every exposed inch of skin as if discovering it for the first time.

"I'm…" She gasped as he took off her bra and cupped her breast. "I'm grateful…for you, too." Trembling with anticipation, she managed to unbutton his shirt, but that was as far as she got before he short-circuited her brain with another soul-deep kiss.

He finished undressing her the same way he'd started, as if she were a long-awaited gift. Then he laid her gently on the bed, moved back and gazed at her while he stripped off his clothes.

"We have light this time," he murmured. Climbing in beside her, he cupped her face and brushed his thumb over her cheek. "I've missed it. Missed being able to see you. Mostly your eyes."

"My eyes? Really?"

"Yes, ma'am. They're pretty all the time, but when I'm inside you they turn a gorgeous dark green, like…like a forest at twilight."

"Wow. That's beautiful."

"No, *you're* beautiful." He brushed a kiss over her mouth. "That's what I'm trying to say, but words don't do you justice. I can't—"

"Then show me."

"Great idea."

Words don't do you justice. He'd given her a dizzying high that wouldn't wear off anytime soon.

He retrieved a condom from the bedside table drawer and put it on before sliding effortlessly into her throbbing channel. She moaned with pleasure.

Holding very still, he gazed down at her. "So special."

"Mm-hm." The hot intensity in his eyes stole her breath. But more than passion filled those brown depths. Caring, acceptance, respect— each touched her heart with a gentle caress, soothing the lonely ache she'd steadfastly ignored since her parents' death. *Safe.*

Slowly he began to move, his gaze never leaving hers. "Let the celebration begin."

"I like the way you party." She grasped his hips and matched his steady rhythm.

"Good." The glow in his eyes grew stronger. "How I love looking at you. You get all pink. Your cheeks, your breasts…" He subtly increased the pace.

"All because of you." She gasped as he rotated his hips, then did it again. "*Luke.*"

"Like that?"

"Yes." She began to pant as he continued his devastatingly effective motion. "And I don't want to come yet."

"Why not?"

She trembled, resisting the urge to surrender to her climax. "I don't want it to be over."

"It won't be. Let go, sweet Abby."

She had no choice. He bore down and she erupted. Then he continued to move, taking her on the rollercoaster a second time.

He loved her so thoroughly that she lost track of where her body ended and his began. He became part of her and she a part of him.

His eyes darkened and he pushed deep. "*Abby.*"

She ignited. Gasping, he shuddered in the grip of his release as they plunged over the edge...together.

So much pleasure. She closed her eyes in gratitude. When she opened them, he was gazing at her with a soft smile.

I love you. She drew in a breath, heart beating fast. It was time. Time to say the words.

A soft whine at the door drew his attention. He glanced toward it. "I guess she misses us."

Maybe not the time, after all. "I'll bet she does."

He leaned down and kissed her gently. "That was wonderful."

"Sure was."

"I'd better go check on the pup." He eased away from her.

"Ready for some dinner?"

"You bet."

After he'd pulled on his jeans and a shirt and she'd slipped into her robe, he opened the door and greeted a very happy Delilah.

The dog curled up in a corner of the kitchen with a chew toy while they put together a quick dinner of leftover meatloaf, salad and steamed veggies. Then she carried the toy into the dining nook and settled there when they sat down to eat.

Luke glanced toward the corner where she gnawed on her toy. "The uncertainty is over, but I still can't quite believe it."

"You will. Might take a few days." His happiness brought her such joy.

He picked up his fork. "After we eat, I'll call my folks and Kendra."

"Great idea. They'll want to know."

"Which reminds me. Mom invited you to have dinner on Sunday night when Hayley comes home. Would you like to?"

Her breath caught. If his mother wanted to include her in a family event, her status had changed.

"You look a little freaked out. If you'd rather not, then—"

"No, I want to. I just...we haven't talked about where we go from here, after my files are organized. Maybe we should."

He put down his fork. "Okay."

"I love having you here, but meanwhile you're not spending time in that house you wanted so much."

"I know." He reached over and took her hand. "But I can't ask you to drive out there and back every night, either, especially this time of year."

"How about a compromise? I'll spend Saturday nights at your house and you can spend two nights here, maybe Tuesday and Thursday."

"Three nights. Tuesday, Wednesday and Thursday. That leaves only three nights we'll be apart and four we'll be together." He squeezed her hand. "Better ratio."

She smiled. "I won't complain about having an extra night with you."

"But I'll probably complain about the nights I'm not with you, so be prepared."

"We'll just enjoy each other even more because we won't have every night together."

"Go ahead and rationalize if you want, but I'll miss you like crazy. So will Delilah."

"I'll miss you, too," she said gently. "But this makes more sense than you staying here all the time."

He sighed. "I'll accept that for now. Just know that I'll be working on alternate solutions. Can we start the program this Saturday night?"

"Love to."

"If you bring a change of clothes, we can go from there to my folks' house for the family dinner on Sunday."

"Sounds great." Their relationship was becoming more defined, and that in turn had inspired the most amazing idea. She wouldn't bring it up tonight, though.

Instead she'd let it simmer, perhaps refine the concept. Then she'd present it to him Saturday evening while they sipped wine in front of a crackling fire. He was going to love it.

25

Luke considered himself an adequate cook, but he wanted something special for Saturday night. Michael Murphy had recently added Irish stew to the menu, so Luke ordered two large servings and stopped by the GG to pick them up on the way to the bakery.

Although traditionally made with mutton or lamb, the GG version of Irish stew featured beef. Michael had bowed to the preferences of the residents of cowboy country. Consequently, his stew had become a hit.

Just shy of four in the afternoon, the Guzzling Grizzly was quiet. Luke walked in and found Michael behind the bar, preparing for the Saturday night crowd.

He flashed Luke his usual cheerful smile. "Got your order right here." He reached over the polished wooden surface and shook Luke's hand. "Where's Delilah?"

"Guarding the truck."

"Yeah?"

"I've been reading up on border collies and they're happiest when they have a job. They like to feel useful."

"Don't we all. It's so cool that you get to keep her."

"Sure is."

"Hey, I'm implementing what we talked about but I have a couple of questions. Got time next week?"

"You bet. Wednesday?"

"Better not. That's Valentine's Day and we'll be busy."

"So it is." And he hadn't come up with something for Abby, yet. "How about Thursday?"

"Thursday works. Can you make it before we open, like ten-thirty?"

"I can do that." He took out his phone and added the appointment to his calendar. "I need to start thinking about Valentine's Day."

"Got a great dinner menu planned for that night." Michael lifted the bag of food onto the counter. "But if you decide on takeout, be sure and get your name on the list by Monday."

"I will. Thanks." He took cash from his wallet. "I don't think Abigail's tried the stew yet. I think she'll really like it."

"Hope so." Michael rang up the purchase. "Have a great weekend."

Luke smiled. "Planning on it."

Abby was ready with a small duffel, a loaf of bread to go with the stew and oatmeal raisin cookies for dessert. He couldn't wait to get her out to his house. And—might as well admit it—into his bed.

Once she was in the truck with Delilah sandwiched between them, his world was complete. He backed out of the parking space.

She took an appreciative sniff. "Something smells delicious."

"It's me. New cologne. Guaranteed to get the ladies hot."

"Is it called Eau de Irish Stew?"

"Matter of fact, it is."

"Perfect choice. I've been wanting to try the GG's new special." She wrapped an arm around Delilah and kneaded her fingers in the dog's ruff. "Hey, doggie. It'll be fun going to your house for a change."

"I told her we were changing the venue and she's almost as happy about having you come out to the house as I am."

"I have you both beat. I'm the happiest of all. You two have a great place. I can't wait to see how the living room looks with the refinished floor and the furniture in there."

"It's a definite improvement. If it's okay with you, I'd like to eat in there instead of using the dining room."

"Works for me. And FYI, I have a business issue I'm dying to discuss."

"What's that?"

"I'll wait until we have a glass of wine for toasting."

"Sounds promising."

She glanced over at him and smiled. "It is. Extremely promising."

"Can't wait to hear about it. The fire's laid, so we could have some wine while the stew's heating. Then you can tell me your promising idea." If she'd come up with another way to increase revenue, so much the better. "Does it have to do with sandwiches?"

"No."

"Soup?"

"No. I doubt you'll guess it, although it's obvious. I don't know why I didn't think of it before."

"Now I'm really curious." And encouraged that she seemed to be thinking like a businesswoman.

He pulled up in front of the house and they hurried inside. After feeding Delilah and putting the stew on to warm, they settled in front of the fire with glasses of wine. Delilah finished her dinner and joined them, curling up on her favorite rag rug.

Abby gazed around the room. "Very nice. The floor looks beautiful."

"Getting the furniture back in here made a big difference, too." He turned toward her. "Okay. Let's hear your idea."

Her eyes sparkled. "You'll love it."

"I'm sure I will."

"Well." She scooted around and tucked one foot under her so she was facing him. "We get along really great."

"We do." He smiled because she was clearly excited about this.

"And we have skills that complement each other. I'm a terrific baker and you're a terrific business manager."

"Also true."

"But running the business isn't my strength."

"Not yet, but you've made a lot of progress. Pretty soon you'll be comfortable wearing both hats."

"But I don't have to." She could barely sit still and her face glowed with eagerness. "Not if I have a business partner who can wear one of them."

His stomach bottomed out. Maybe he'd misunderstood. He hoped to God he had. "Are you talking about me?"

"Of course, silly!"

"Oh, Abby."

She looked as if he'd slapped her. "What do you mean saying *oh, Abby* like that? Like you wish I hadn't said it."

"I wish you hadn't."

"Why? It's a logical progression! We'd make a great team! We'd..." She gulped and fell silent. "You hate it."

"I don't hate it." He reached over and took her hand. "But it's not for me."

"Why not? We work well together. You could handle the finances and marketing and I could handle the baking. We'd each be capitalizing on what we do best!"

"I have my own business."

"But you just got started. And you could still do that on the side while we—"

"No, Abby. I worked in the food industry before. That's not my dream. I want to travel, to help business owners all over the state, maybe use Badger Air if I get clients who are too far away to justify driving."

She was heartbroken. Everything about her telegraphed it—slumped shoulders, trembling hands, shallow breathing.

"Abby, I'm so sorry." He rubbed her cold hand. "I'll do everything I can to help you create a system to handle your business, but I don't want to handle it for you. I don't even believe in that. You need to know what's going on. That gives you power."

Her gaze was that of a wounded animal. "I don't want power. I want you."

"You can have me. Just not as a business partner." He'd blown her out of the water. He hated that, but he couldn't go along with her plan. It wasn't fair to either of them. He needed to teach her how to handle the business on her own. "Tell you what. Let's have some dinner. Later I can boot up my computer and show you a spreadsheet that would be great for—"

"I'm not hungry."

Oh, boy. "Abby, I'm sorry. I know you're disappointed, but—"

"Since you're not interested in being my business partner, the best thing you can do for me right now is take me home."

"Abby..."

"No, really, Luke. I was so sure you'd go for this and...I need time. Please take me home."

Kendra had been right. She was rejecting his advice, and him along with it. And he couldn't figure out a single way to stop it. "Okay." First he smothered the fire as best he could. It would have to do. At the last minute, he remembered to turn off the stove. Then he fetched their coats and got

Delilah's leash. "Come on, pup. We're going for a ride."

The dog took her time getting up from her cozy spot on the rug.

"I'm sorry, Delilah." Abby walked over and leaned down to kiss the top of her head. "But I wouldn't be very good company tonight."

The trip back was silent except for the breathing of two people and a dog. Luke reached for the knob on the radio and pulled his hand back. Music wasn't going to help.

Nothing was going to help unless he agreed to be her business partner. He couldn't do that. It wouldn't be good for him and it would be terrible for her.

Outside the door to her apartment building, he told Delilah to guard the truck while he walked Abby to the door. "We'll work this out." He said it as much to reassure himself as to comfort her.

"I hope so, Luke." Her expression was bereft as she looked up at him.

"Take some time. Call me when you're ready to talk."

She nodded, although she hadn't exactly agreed to call him. "See you later."

He waited as she unlocked the deadbolt and pushed on the door. It didn't open.

"Here, let me—"

"I've got it." She rammed it with her shoulder. Didn't budge. "Stupid door!"

"Abby, stand back. I'll get it."

"Thanks." Scowling, she crossed her arms and moved away from the door.

Luke took hold of the knob, braced his shoulder against the door and shoved hard. The door banged open and he stumbled into the entryway as Roxanne appeared at the top of the stairs.

"Luke! What the hell?" Roxanne stared at him in confusion. "Where's Abigail?"

"I'm here." She came in behind him. "I couldn't get the door open."

Ingrid came up behind Roxanne. "What are you guys doing here? You're supposed to be at Luke's house."

"Long story," Abigail said.

"Where's Delilah?"

"In the truck." Luke tipped his hat. "'Night ladies." He turned to Abby. "Stay in touch." And he walked out the door, closing it behind him.

He climbed behind the wheel and waited until his breathing slowed before turning the key. He desperately needed to swear a blue streak, but that would only upset Delilah. She already looked worried as hell.

He scrubbed a hand over her head. "It'll work out, girl." He wasn't sure, but it was something to say. "Let's go home."

26

Abigail took a deep breath and glanced up at her friends. "You're probably wondering what's going on."

"I sure am." Roxanne looked concerned.

"But if you don't want to talk about it, we'll understand," Ingrid said.

"On the other hand," Roxanne said, "talking is very therapeutic. Venting to sympathetic listeners over a bottle of wine beats sobbing your eyes out in your lonely apartment. Just my two cents."

"Rox has a point. And wine."

"I don't feel like sobbing. I feel like screaming."

"Then come up and scream," Roxanne said. "We can take it."

"I won't scream. But I wouldn't mind venting, now that you mention it." She locked the door and started up the stairs.

"Venting is excellent when you've had a fight with your boyfriend," Ingrid said.

"Except we didn't fight." She might have raised her voice a time or two, but he never had.

Roxanne looked puzzled. "Then what's going on?"

"What's going on is that Luke, in his typically polite way, just tore my dream to shreds."

"Damn, girlfriend." Roxanne wrapped an arm around her shoulders and guided her into the apartment. "You sound pissed."

"You would be, too, if the man you lo—" She gulped. "I mean *like*."

"No, you had it right the first time. You're in love with him." Roxanne turned to Ingrid. "Agreed?"

"Definitely."

Abigail sighed. "Yeah, might as well admit it. I love the jerk, which makes it all worse."

"If he's been a jerk to you, then he's dead to me." Ingrid handed her a tumbler full of wine. "Drink up and tell us all about it."

Over way too much wine, Abigail explained her great idea and Luke's immediate dismissal of the concept. "I offered him a full partnership and he didn't even have the courtesy to say he'd think about it. Or the good sense. It's a great offer, right?"

"It's a great offer." Ingrid refilled her wine glass. "But—"

"But he can't see that! I know!"

"He already has a business, though," Roxanne said.

Ingrid nodded. "That's what I was going to say."

"But he's just starting it. It's not like I'm asking him to give up something he's thoroughly into."

Roxanne picked up her wine glass. "I'm probably the wrong person to comment. I love being a sole proprietor. I can't imagine taking on a partner or worse yet, agreeing to be a partner in someone else's business."

"I can see how you'd feel that way, but Luke already acts kind of like a partner in my business. We've worked together for several weeks, now."

"Not quite the same as being co-owners." Roxanne took a sip of wine.

"Maybe not, but I think it would work out well for both of us. Instead he said it wasn't right for him and wasn't right for me, either. How would he know?"

Ingrid swirled the wine in her glass. "Maybe I had the wrong idea about why you hired him. I thought he was supposed to offer guidance so you could get a better handle on running the business."

"Well...yeah, but if he's really good at that part, and I'm really good at the baking, then—"

"Sweetie, that's short-term thinking." Roxanne put down her glass and leaned forward. "This may sound morbid, but what if he agreed to be your partner and then something happened to him?"

Her insides twisted.

"I can see you hate the thought and I don't blame you. But delegating the business side to someone else leaves you vulnerable. You'd likely lose your bakery, too, because you wouldn't know how to run it by yourself."

She stared into her wine glass. She of all people knew that life was unpredictable. Dealing with her grief after her parents' death had been hard enough. Handling the details of wills and probate had been worse, in a way. It had dragged on for five long years because until then she'd kept herself blissfully ignorant of such matters.

Before Luke had come into the picture, her business had been in dire straits for the same reason. She'd embraced blissful ignorance and made herself vulnerable.

His advice and support had helped turn things around, but...Roxanne had a point, damn it. Which meant Luke might have one, too. Now there was a bitter pill.

She glanced up at Roxanne. "The thought of creating a spreadsheet gives me hives."

"I'd offer to teach you, but I think you'd learn faster using the book I have. The explanations are super simple."

"Could I please borrow it for a little while?"

"You bet."

* * *

A funny thing happened the next morning when Abigail took Roxanne's book down to her office. Creating a spreadsheet on her computer gave her a thrill. She and Luke had organized her receipts into neat manila envelopes and she brought a stack of those down.

Entering data took concentration and she messed up a few times, but Roxanne's book helped her fix her mistakes. She hated to admit it, but turning the paper receipts into something she could scan at a glance was sort of cool.

She worked all day and past her usual bedtime. The following day she used any spare moments to pop into her office and continue entering data.

At closing time, Ingrid asked how things were going.

"Not too bad. I wouldn't say this is the easiest thing I've ever done."

"I can tell. But I think it's great that you're diving in."

She took a deep breath. "I need to. Until I talked with you guys, I just wasn't getting it. This is my business, which means keeping track of the finances. I can't hand that off."

"No, you can't." Ingrid gave her a hug. "Just remember that Roxanne and I are there for you if you need us."

"I know you are and that's awesome. But I need to climb this mountain by myself."

"I understand." She hesitated. "What about Luke?"

"I'm still thinking."

"Gotcha. See you tomorrow, then." She grabbed her coat and left.

Luke. Abigail's chest tightened. She missed everything about him. He had the best smile.

And the best laugh. It could be either happy or toe-curling sexy depending on his mood.

Sometimes he was teasing and sometimes tender. His joy when he'd found out Delilah would stay with him had been...epic.

Then there was Delilah. That cute face, those expressive eyes. Her enthusiasm for life.

What to do about Luke? Nothing for now. She had data to enter. Once again she worked past her usual bedtime and again throughout the day on Tuesday.

After the bakery closed, she got a call from the hardware store. Delilah's tag was ready. She'd completely forgotten ordering it.

She picked up the red metal heart and then stood in the hardware store staring at it and blinking back tears. Delilah's name was engraved on the front and Luke's name and number were on the back.

She'd intended it to be part of a Valentine's gift—a big heart-shaped oatmeal raisin cookie for Luke and an identification tag for Delilah. He'd talked about getting her one so she'd never be lost again. Now what to do with it? Tucking it in her pocket, she went back to Pie in the Sky.

That night she finished the data entry. She printed it out, two copies for added peace of mind. It was in the computer and on a backup drive. After all that work, she didn't want to lose a single digit.

Triumphant, she held the printed version in her hand. She'd done it, by God. She'd climbed the mountain and taken control of her finances. It was a huge victory.

And hadn't Luke promised it would be? Hadn't he said she'd be happy once she'd accomplished this?

He'd been right. And she'd been wrong. Humbling, indeed. Her misplaced anger had created the divide that separated them. Owning up to that wouldn't be easy. She sighed. One challenge down, one to go.

Valentine's Day dawned clear and cold. The shop was crazy busy with all hands on deck, but she made sure that sales were recorded and inventory tracked. The new regime was in place. Ingrid's *Love at First Sight* coffee drink brought in a boatload of money.

Abigail gave Doug and Yolanda big hugs at the end of the day and sent them home. Then she collapsed into a bistro chair across from where Ingrid was sitting with two mugs of *Love at First Sight* coffee.

"Because we deserve it." She raised her cup. "To you, Abigail."

"To you, Ingrid."

"Roxanne and I are going over to the Guzzling Grizzly for the Valentine's bash tonight. Want to come?"

"No, thanks."

"I'm just curious. Did you get Luke a gift?"

"I got Delilah a gift." She described it.

"Aw! That's precious. You need to take it over there. Doesn't have to be today, I guess."

She gazed at her friend. "I think it does. I think it's time for this girl to admit she's been wrong."

Ingrid went into spasms of joy. "Drink your coffee and get out of here, then. But what are you giving Luke? I mean, aside from the obvious, lots of nookie."

"I'll show you." Leaving the table, she went into her office and came back with the heart-shaped bakery boxes they'd special-ordered because they looked so classy.

"Bakery items are always a hit."

"It isn't a bakery item." She opened it and showed Ingrid the contents.

"Oh, my God, you do know that man. Okay, now leave, leave right now. I'll finish up here."

"Okay. Thanks." She hurried upstairs to fetch the tag and hopped in her SUV. What if he wasn't home? She could text him. No. She wouldn't have the slightest idea what to say in a text.

The drive seemed to take forever, but at last she pulled up in front of his house. Smoke drifted up from the chimney. He was home.

Delilah's bark sounded from inside the house and he came out on the porch with her by his side. He was so beautiful she teared up. They were both beautiful. She'd almost blown her chance at something wonderful.

When she climbed out, Delilah dashed toward her, tongue out, tail going a mile-a-minute. Luke called her back, but she paid no attention.

Abigail tucked the box under her arm and crouched down. "I've missed you, girl." Her voice was a little wobbly as she stroked the dog's silky head. "Missed you so much."

Then she stood and faced the man standing on the porch. He hadn't bothered to put on a jacket. He had to be cold, but he held his ground.

As well he should. She walked toward him, Delilah prancing by her side. "Happy Valentine's Day."

He didn't respond, but his gaze locked with hers. She couldn't read it.

"You were right."

He cleared his throat. "About what?"

"Me taking control of my own finances, my own business." She climbed the steps and held out the box. "This is for you. You can keep it or throw it in the fire. I have another copy plus a backup on my computer."

He took the heart-shaped box and opened it. His eyes widened. Then he pulled out the printed sheets. "You did this?"

"Yep. Roxanne loaned me her book, but I did it all myself."

"Congratulations."

She could read his expression, now. His eyes glowed with warmth and...dared she believe something more? "Thank you. I, um, have something else, something for Delilah." She took the tag out of her pocket, put it in her palm and held it out to him.

He glanced down. His throat moved and he looked up again. "Abby..."

"I know you were thinking of getting one, but if this isn't right, or you've already—"

"I haven't." He sounded a little hoarse. He tucked the spreadsheets back in the box, took the metal tag and put that in before closing the flaps. "Do you want to come in?"

"That would be nice."

He opened the door and waited for her to go through. Delilah followed, beside herself with excitement.

After walking in, he set the box on the coffee table before turning to her. "Before you say anything else, there's something you need to know."

Her stomach churned. He looked so serious. Had her behavior ruined what they had, after all? Was he going to ask her to leave? Well, she would, but she wouldn't give up hope. They'd had something great and they could still—

"I needed time to think, but if you hadn't come out here tonight, I was planning to come to you on Saturday."

"Oh." To break up with her for good? Anxiety made her tremble.

"I don't want to be your business partner, but—" He paused and took a deep breath. "I'm hoping we can still build a life together."

She stared at him in bewilderment. He wasn't angry with her. Instead he—

"I love you, Abby."

Her vision blurred and she pressed a hand to her chest. She was shaking so bad she didn't know if she'd be able to get the words out.

But she had to. He needed to hear them. "I...l-love y-you, t-too."

"Thank God." In two strides, he was there and his mouth covered hers.

That was all it took for her world to make sense—the warmth of his love, the shelter of his arms...and the magic of his kiss.

Michael Murphy needs the luck of the Irish to convince Roxanne Sawyer she should take a chance on love in A COWBOY'S LUCK, book eight in the McGavin Brothers series!

* * * * *

Roxanne wanted to blame her crazy heartbeat on rushing over here. Except she'd driven instead of hotfooting it for six blocks, so that excuse didn't wash. Might as well face it—Michael Murphy lit a fire under her every time she looked at him.

Today he'd worn a moss green shirt that exactly matched his eyes. He wore green a lot, claiming it was an Irish thing. Maybe he was oblivious to how it drew attention to those amazing eyes.

He might not realize how perfectly he fit the cowboy ideal dressed in jeans, boots, and a yoked shirt. Feasting her gaze on Michael was like walking into an art museum—so much beauty that she had trouble deciding where to focus her attention.

Bryce was in the office texting on his phone. He glanced up. "Hey, Roxanne! That was fast."

"Couldn't wait to see these T-shirts."

"Then let's end the suspense." Michael handed her the box cutter.

She sliced through the tape and tugged open the flaps before digging out the tissue-wrapped shirts. Tossing each of the guys a package, she unwrapped a man's crew neck. They'd ordered one for Michael and one for Bryce.

She shook it out. "I like it. Material feels good and the white logo looks *really* good against the black."

"Let's see how it fits."

Roxanne's head came up as snaps popped. Surely Michael wasn't...oh, yes, he was! He stripped off his shirt and flung it across the back of the desk chair. She almost swallowed her tongue.

Pecs bulging...flexing...sweet heaven! Time slowed as he reached for the T-shirt and pulled it over his head. Then he shoved his arms into the sleeves one at a time. *Abs tightening...shirt descending... covering...no!* She prayed she hadn't protested out loud.

"What do you guys think?" His grin wasn't the least self-conscious. Evidently he had no clue he'd just fried her circuits. "Does it work?"

Bryce looked up from his phone. "Fits great, buddy. Just don't wash it in hot water."

"Exactly." She licked dry lips and coaxed words from tight vocal cords. "You can't afford to have it shrink." *Lest your female customers spontaneously combust.* They might, anyway.

The Guzzling Grizzly logo had looked good on her computer screen, even better on the antique mirror behind the bar, and striking against the black cotton T-shirt material. But it had never enjoyed a more eye-popping venue than the muscled chest of Michael Murphy.

*New York Times bestselling author Vicki Lewis
Thompson's love affair with cowboys started with
the Lone Ranger, continued through Maverick, and
took a turn south of the border with Zorro. She
views cowboys as the Western version of knights in
shining armor, rugged men who value honor,
honesty and hard work. Fortunately for her, she
lives in the Arizona desert, where broad-shouldered,
lean-hipped cowboys abound. Blessed with such an
abundance of inspiration, she only hopes that she
can do them justice.*

*For more information about this prolific author,
visit her website and sign up for her newsletter. She
loves connecting with readers.*

VickiLewisThompson.com

CPSIA information can be obtained
at www.ICGtesting.com
Printed in the USA
LVHW012255160520
655784LV00001B/53